BEST OF THE BEST
DETECTIVE STORIES
25th ANNIVERSARY COLLECTION

BEST OF THE BEST DETECTIVE STORIES
25th ANNIVERSARY COLLECTION

Edited by Allen J. Hubin

E. P. DUTTON & CO., INC.　NEW YORK · 1971

Contents

6 | Contents

Introduction

In March of 1945 David C. Cooke came to John Tebbel, an editor at E. P. Dutton & Co., with a suggestion for a series of anthologies of short tales of crime and detection, the best that could be culled from the hundreds (indeed, in those early years, thousands) published chiefly in magazines during each calendar year. That eminently worthy suggestion was taken up, and for fifteen years, commencing in 1946, Mr. Cooke edited the annual volumes, followed in turn by Brett Halliday (two years), Anthony Boucher (six years) and myself (two years). Over the years tens of thousands of short stories have been examined with some diligence to sift out the finest (a checklist of the 334 stories so chosen may be found at the end of this volume). Thus the series of *Best Detective Stories of the Year* may reasonably lay some claim to being the most important permanent general repository for the modern crime story.

The present volume is conceived as a tribute to the first twenty-five years of *Best Detective Stories of the Year,* and it fell to my considerable pleasure—not unmixed with a little pain, as you shall shortly see—to be its editor. The ground rules were simple: to select from each of the volumes one premier tale, while not re-using any of the fourteen selections reprinted in a *Best of the Best* compilation published in 1960, nor any of the twenty-four in *Boucher's Choicest,* published in 1969 to commemorate the late Anthony Boucher's skillful and imaginative editorship.

Reading through that quarter century of short stories was at once an exhilarating and sobering experience. Exhilarating—because the stories were polished and gloriously varied in theme and treatment. Sobering—because of writers gone and, in their own special ways, irreplaceable; and because I seemed to sense with the unfolding of the years a certain loss of innocence (a subtle loss, for example, in the depiction of policemen).

As if to compensate, however, the generally humor-free substance of the earlier anthologies—Craig Rice's sunny larks are the only notable exception—came to be leavened with a lively sense of the absurd, a development that was most evident in the years under Boucher's editorship. You will find something both of lost innocence and of newfound humor in the pages that follow.

The pain I mentioned earlier was one of selection. In many cases I was faced with a choice between two or three superior candidates for a single year—and how could any of them be left out, as in fact they must? Read—if you can—the original twenty-five volumes in chronological order. But if you are not blessed with a full row on your shelves, read the tales which follow, and catch a glimpse of the sweeping tapestry of short crime fiction, of approaches gone and new freedoms realized, yet all confirming the old truth that a story well told exerts undying fascination.

BEST OF THE **BEST**
DETECTIVE STORIES
25th ANNIVERSARY COLLECTION

This chilling story from the maiden volume in the Best Detective *series has several surprises in store. It's not often given unto a man to solve his own murder . . .*

BRUNO FISCHER

The Man Who Lost His Head

The woman looked at Jim Crane and screamed. She had come out of the tall brick house which he had just passed.

Crane stopped under the streetlamp and looked around. There was nobody else on that dark, empty street. The brick house stood off by itself, flanked by lots. He turned back to the woman.

"What's the matter?" he asked.

She cowered in the doorway. Her voice had stopped with that one shrill outcry, but her mouth continued to hang open. She pointed jerkily at him with a forefinger.

"You—your—" she gasped.

Fright had driven her into almost speechless hysteria. Could she be frightened of him? That was crazy. He was sure he had never before seen this dumpy, middle-aged woman.

"What's wrong?" he said, going toward her.

She put out her hands as if to ward him off, and again she screamed.

Overhead a voice shouted: "Hey, you, keep away from her!"

A man in his undershirt was sticking his head out of a second-floor window. The woman was whimpering now.

"What the devil is going on?" Crane demanded.

"You beat it!" the man said. "You want me to call a cop?"

Both the woman and the man were mad, Crane told himself. If a cop arrived, it would be tough explaining that he hadn't tried to harm the woman in any way. People always took a woman's word against a man's. Best to get away from here.

He sent his long legs down the street. When he had gone a short distance, he looked back. The woman had come all the way out on the sidewalk and was staring after him. Crane wanted none of her; she seemed capable of chasing after him with wild accusations.

He was hurrying around the corner house when he heard the woman say in a loud, cracked voice: "Did you see him, Mr. Prim?"

"Sure I saw him." That was doubtless the man at the window replying. "Luckily I heard you and looked out and chased him off."

"I don't mean that. The poor man. He frightened me so."

Crane had not stopped walking. He could still hear the voices on the other street, but no longer the words. She was nuts, all right. What had she said? *"The poor man. He frightened me so."* That wasn't sane talk. You met all kinds of people during a walk.

He stopped. A walk? He wasn't out for a walk. He had left his house to call on Ellen Hoyt, but this wasn't the way. This street and the other he had been on when the woman had screamed were unfamiliar.

He reached the farther intersection and looked up at the signpost. The motion of his head made his stomach churn, and he wondered why that should be. Then he forgot about his stomach when he saw that he was on the corner of Washington Avenue and Fourth Street.

Ellen Hoyt lived on Washington Avenue, but near Tenth Street. And he himself lived farther uptown. Ellen's apartment was between his home and where he now was. How in the world had he gone six blocks past his destination?

He stood at the signpost trying to remember. He had come home from his office and showered and shaved and left to take Ellen out to dinner. On pleasant evenings like this he preferred walking. But he didn't recall walking. He couldn't recall anything after having left his house until the woman in the doorway had screamed.

So he had been dreaming while strolling along, probably thinking of next month when he and Ellen would be married. He had passed Ellen's house without knowing it. Some time or other that happened to everybody. No use brooding about it.

Jim Crane crossed the street and headed toward Tenth Street. His stomach felt queasy. It had started, he remembered, when he had brought his head all the way back to look up at the signpost. His legs felt wobbly too. What was the matter with him? Had the woman's screams upset him?

A neon sign ahead read: COFFEE. He decided that what was wrong with him was merely hunger. He had had a very light lunch at twelve, and now it was around seven-thirty. A cup of coffee would hold him until he and Ellen got to the restaurant.

The lunchroom was small and grimy and deserted except for a burly counterman reading a racing form. Crane slid onto a counter stool and reached for his cigarettes.

"Coffee," he said.

The counterman looked up from his paper. He frowned. "You feel all right, mister?"

"I—" Crane was feeling a lot better now that he was sitting. "Of course I'm all right," he said testily. "Why?"

"Well, you look sort of green."

Crane chuckled. "That's what comes of being an accountant. Too much indoor work. Mind rushing that coffee? I'm late."

The counterman looked sharply at him and then turned to the coffee urn. Behind the counter there was a flyspecked mirror which had been blocked off by the counterman's broad body. Now Crane saw himself in it, sitting hunched forward with his hat pulled low over his forehead and a cigarette dangling from his thin mouth. His long, angular face, he thought, looked like a death's head. He had never cared for his face, but Ellen said she loved it. But now it was pinched more than usual, and his complexion, which had always been sallow, was actually green.

I hope I'm not coming down with any sickness, he thought, and glanced at the wall clock over the door. It said twenty to eleven.

"Your clock's fast," he told the counterman as the coffee was set down before him.

"Maybe a couple of minutes."

"You mean three hours," Crane said and looked at his wristwatch. The hands read the same as those on the wall clock.

It couldn't be. He had left at seven-fifteen to reach Ellen's apartment at seven-thirty. He had gone out of his way, so maybe he was a few minutes late. But three hours? And without remembering a single minute of those hours?

In the mirror he saw fear spring into his eyes. "Listen," he said tensely. "Is this Friday, October twenty-seventh?"

The counterman's brows creased. "Sure it is, mister. Say, you're as sick as you look if you ain't even sure what day it is."

Crane sighed. At least it wasn't amnesia or anything like that. But three hours lost!

Then he thought he had the answer. For some reason he had read the clock hands wrong. Not twenty to eleven, but five to eight. He turned his head to again look at the wall clock. He had been right the first time; it was the hour hand which was almost on the eleven.

"Holy God!" the counterman cried. "What happened to you, mister?"

"Eh?"

Crane took his eyes from the clock. The counterman was racing around the counter. In bewilderment, Crane watched him.

"Your head!" The counterman stepped behind Crane, and his voice was shrill with horror. "Holy God!"

Crane put a hand to the back of his neck. He felt the short hairs at the nape matted as if stuck with glue.

"Blood?" he muttered incredulously.

"It's all over the back of your jacket and—" The counterman's eyes bulged. "Jeez, don't you feel nothing, mister?"

"Why, no," Crane said slowly. "I felt a little sick to my stomach a little while ago, but it's gone away. It must be just a flesh wound."

"A flesh wound!" The counterman's manner suddenly became gentle and anxious. "Now don't you move, mister. Stay right where you are. Just you sit there while I call an ambulance."

"Oh, come," Crane said in annoyance. "It can't be much if I don't feel it. I'll wash up at my girl friend's place."

"You stay where you are." The counterman dug a coin out of his apron and rushed to the phone booth. When he was inside, he stuck his head out. "Don't get off that chair, mister. Don't try walking. Take it easy."

Crane scowled into his coffee. One thing was clear: the blow on his head was responsible for the three lost hours. But he couldn't remember what had happened. Had he fallen? Had somebody socked him and taken his money?

He fished out his wallet. Twenty-eight dollars—check. He had had nothing else of value on his person. So it had to be a fall. But where and how?

In the phone booth the counterman was saying: "Yeah, on Washington, right off Fifth. And you better hurry."

What was the guy getting so excited about? So he had lost a little blood. The wound couldn't amount to much because he didn't feel any after-effects. Again Crane put his hand up to the back of his neck. Nothing there except dried blood. His hand started to move up.

That was when the street door opened and a thick-set, swarthy man came in. He started to close the door behind him and then froze. He gaped at Crane; his thick lips began to tremble and sweat formed beads on his brow.

Crane swung on his stool so he could face the newcomer directly. He was sure he had never seen him before. Yet this man was as scared of him as the woman in the doorway had been.

"Do you know me?" Crane demanded, getting off the stool.

Crane felt himself shudder. Maybe the woman who had screamed had been frightened by the sight of blood, and the counterman thought he was hurt badly enough to need treatment —but the swarthy man hadn't seen the back of his head. Crane had been turned partly toward him when he had entered.

What *had* happened during those three lost hours? Was the swarthy man in any way connected with the wound?

He moved to the door. Sidelong through the window he saw the swarthy man standing thirty feet beyond the store and looking back. He seemed to be hesitating over something.

Anger gripped Crane. He'd get to the bottom of this. He'd make the swarthy man tell him why he was afraid of him.

He flung the door open. The counterman came out of the booth and yelled: "Hey, mister, for God's sake! The ambulance's coming! Don't—"

Crane kept going.

The moment the swarthy man saw Crane appear in the street, he started walking rapidly uptown. He did not quite run.

"Just a minute," Crane called as he moved after him. "I only want to ask you—"

The swarthy man put his head down and dug his hands into his pockets and pumped his short legs. Crane's longer legs cut down the distance between them.

Then the swarthy man was out of sight around the Sixth Street corner. And when Crane rounded the corner, the other was waiting for him, with his wide shoulders pressed against the wall and a big ugly revolver in his hand.

"Keep away from me!" the swarthy man panted.

Crane blinked down at the gun. He said: "Don't be foolish. I only want to ask you how you happen to know me."

There wasn't much light, but Crane could see the other's face strained in fear. It didn't look like a face that frightened easily. It was a hard and cruel and ruthless face—or had been up to a minute ago.

"You're dead!" the swarthy man whimpered. "Don't touch me!"

Everybody he had met in the last few minutes was stark, raving mad, Crane told himself. Or maybe it was he himself who had lost his reason. He had to know. He decided to humor him.

"How do you know I'm dead?" Crane said. "If you never saw me before—"

The gun jerked up, and for the first time Crane realized the full menace of it. The damn idiot would actually shoot!

"You can't trick me," the swarthy man said hoarsely. "You want me to say right out how I know you're dead. You want to make sure. Well, this time *I'll* make sure." And his hand contracted about the trigger of the gun.

There was a feeble click. Nothing else.

The swarthy man looked down at his gun. Then he looked up into Crane's face. With a choked cry, he dashed past Crane and wildly up the street.

Crane remained rooted to the spot, watching the flight of that stocky shape until it was out of sight. He did not try to follow. He was afraid of a gun which unaccountably had not killed him. And he was afraid of more than a gun—of something he did not understand or even know, but that now was becoming a dim, nagging memory in back of his consciousness.

A siren sounded and then an ambulance swept past him. Looking around the corner, he saw it come to a stop in front of the lunchroom. The ambulance was for him.

He hurried in the opposite direction. The wound wasn't important enough to delay him. Ellen was probably sore at him for not having shown up. Or worried. He had to get to her at once.

But Ellen was dead.

His breath came out in a sobbing gasp. He stopped walking and then resumed almost at once. What had made that absurd thought pop into his head? He had spoken to her on the phone at six o'clock this evening. He had had a date with her at seven-thirty, but he hadn't reached her apartment because something had happened on the way.

Ellen was dead.

There it was again, a voice inside of him telling him with dreadful certainty.

"No!" he said aloud. "That blow made me sappy; it's making me imagine things."

Ellen lay face down in a pool of her own blood.

"Stop it!" he said fiercely. "She's all right. She's fine. She had a nasty experience this morning, but nothing happened to her and she spoke to you at six o'clock. It's you who were bleeding. It's you who were hurt."

How badly hurt? He seemed to be having no bad physical effects, yet he was having a mental reaction that was giving him terrible thoughts. He felt the back of his head, the dried blood caked at the nape. There should be a cut higher up. His hand moved up almost to the hatband.

There was no skull. His fingers kept going in.

He staggered. His hand jerked away. *I'm dead,* he thought. *That's what scared those people. The top of my head is gone. The swarthy man knew I couldn't be alive.*

He recovered, telling himself that he must have lost sensation in his fingertips. A wound always felt worse than it was.

By the light of a streetlamp he could see his reflection in the window of a clothing store. The collar of his light tweed jacket was smeared with blood; a dried splotch of it trailed between his shoulders. But no matter how he turned, he could not get the back of his head into his line of vision.

He stepped into the store vestibule. The door glass was also like a mirror; it was at an angle with the store window so that he could see the back of his head. He removed his hat.

A section of his skull had sunk into his head, and there was sight of shredded bone where the hair did not cover it. It wasn't bleeding now and had probably not bled enough to have greatly weakened him. Had the blood clotted? Was the horribly pressed-in bone still a covering for the wound? He could not see well, but he had seen enough.

Yet he felt nothing but shock, and shock shook him for a long minute. Then carefully he placed his hat far back on his head, covering the visible bone. He fumbled a cigarette out of his pocket and used half a book of matches.

The screaming of the woman in the doorway now made sense. She had seen the back of his skull when he had passed under the light, and the horror of it had unnerved her. The counterman had retained only a little more self-control. But where did the swarthy man come in? He hadn't seen the wound. Crane had always been facing him.

And Ellen was dead, lying in a pool of her own blood.

No! His mind had been affected by the blow. Desperately he tried to think. He had left his house, and then a woman had screamed. Between, in that period, Ellen lay dead. That was all there was, and it had to be a lie.

He found himself walking, and he was fighting the tremendous urge to rush to the nearest doctor, to the nearest hospital, for a chance to survive. But first he had to see Ellen.

He did not remember covering the few remaining blocks. Suddenly he was inside the apartment house, pressing the button for the automatic elevator. He rode up to the third floor, walked up the hall, turned the corner—and there was a uniformed policeman standing in front of Ellen's door.

His knees started to buckle. The cop leaped forward, grabbed his arm.

"You're hurt?" the cop asked, peering into his face. "You look sick. Say, who are you?"

Crane fought himself erect. "I'm all right. My name is James Crane, and I—"

"We been looking for you," the cop broke in excitedly.

The cop pushed the door open. There were half a dozen men in Ellen's compact one-room apartment. And Ellen was there.

She lay face down on the floor, with her long brown hair spread about her face like a halo. And there was blood in her hair and on the rug—blood which had run out of the hideous hole in her head.

It was like coming back to the scene of a tragedy, where he had been before. Three hours ago, he knew now, he had seen her just like this.

"Crane, eh?" A man with fiery eyes stood in front of him. "I'm Lieutenant Blanchard."

Crane leaned weakly against the wall. "We were to be married next month," he muttered.

A little of it was coming back to Crane. He remembered being inside this apartment three hours ago and staring down at Ellen lying dead in her own blood. He had heard a sound behind him and had started to turn, but he had never had a chance to complete that turn. And then blankness.

Crane said: "The murderer also struck me. Look." He took off his hat and turned his back to the room.

A startled gasp went up from the men. The lieutenant said sharply: "Dr. Rowland!" A chubby-faced man, who was doubtless the coroner, gently took Crane's arm and led him to the couch. Crane lay down and pressed his face to the cushion.

Fingers probed the back of his skull, but seemed to avoid the wound. Dr. Rowland said incredulously: "You mean to say you've been walking around like this?"

"I feel all right," Crane muttered. "Except once when I threw back my head too quickly to look at a signpost. It made me sick to my stomach for a few minutes. Will I be all right?"

"We'll have you fixed up in no time."

Lieutenant Blanchard asked: "Could that wound have been self-inflicted?"

"Nonsense!" Dr. Rowland straightened up. "He was struck from behind."

There was silence then. Even the murmuring of the other men in the room had ceased. Crane turned his face on the cushion and saw that Blanchard and Dr. Rowland had crossed to the other side of the room and were consulting in whispers. But the room was small and disjointed phrases reached him.

". . . nothing I can do here," Dr. Rowland was saying. ". . . hospital . . . even there . . . should have died instantly . . . bone pressing . . ."

His voice got too low. Then Blanchard was speaking and Crane strained to hear.

". . . left here under his own power . . . came back . . . talks all right and . . ."

Dr. Rowland shook his head and his voice rose testily, so that Crane got full sentences.

"It's one of these phenomena medical men can't quite explain. I've come across it before in similar injuries. The person does not even suspect that he is fatally injured. He might feel and act normal for a considerable period, and then suddenly—" Dr. Rowland glanced at Crane and saw how intensely he was listening, and lowered his voice.

Crane buried his head in the cushion. He could finish the doctor's sentence: *and then suddenly drops dead.* He had had a cousin who had received a head injury in an auto accident. His cousin had got up and walked home, acting outwardly normal, and a couple of hours later he had collapsed and died.

The swarthy man was right, Crane thought dully. *I'm dead. But not yet dead enough for him.*

"Lieutenant," he said aloud, "I know who did it. It was the man who held Ellen up this morning."

Blanchard returned to the side of the couch. "What do you know about the holdup?"

"Only what Ellen told me over the phone."

Crane spoke with his eyes closed and the side of his face against the cushion. "Ellen worked for a paper mill, in the office. Among other things, she handled the payroll. It was lunch hour and she was the only one in the office. She was behind in getting the payroll out and planned to have lunch later. She was putting the money into the envelopes when two armed men with handkerchiefs tied over their faces came in. One stayed at the door to watch if anybody came from the plant. The other gathered up the money. As he was about to leave, the knot became untied in his handkerchief and it fell from his face. He shot at Ellen, but missed. She dropped behind a desk. By then there was an uproar outside and the man whose face Ellen had seen couldn't take the time to go around the desk after her. He and the other man fled.

"Late this afternoon Ellen phoned me at my office. She was very upset. She had just come from police headquarters, where she had been shown photos, but she hadn't seen the gunman's. She could describe him only vaguely because he had no outstanding characteristics, but she was sure she would recognize him if she ever saw him again. I told her I'd be over right after work to take her out to dinner and help her get over her terrible experience. At six o'clock I phoned her again. She said she was feeling better. But when I got here at seven-thirty—" Crane's voice broke.

"Go on," Blanchard urged.

"Ellen didn't answer the door when I rang. I found it unlocked. I walked in, and there was Ellen, just the way she is now. Then I heard somebody behind me, and that's all I know." Crane shivered. "I guess after a while I recovered consciousness and picked up my hat and went out, but I don't remember."

"And you didn't see the guy?"

"Not then," Crane said. "But later." And he told about the swarthy man.

Lieutenant Blanchard frowned. "The man she described was tall and rather gaunt."

"Then it was the other man who murdered us," Crane said. One of the detectives in the room uttered an exclamation. Every pair of eyes stared at Crane. He realized what he had said. *Us! The man had murdered us!*

Well, wasn't that the truth?

He wet his lips and went on: "The swarthy man must have been the gunman whose face Ellen didn't see. In fact, he was mostly outside the door during the holdup, so she hadn't even been able to describe his build. But he was the one who murdered her."

Gravely Blanchard nodded. "It's likely."

Crane got up on one elbow and felt bitterness choke him. "Damn you, didn't you know she'd be in danger? Wasn't she entitled to police protection?"

Blanchard said quietly, "She didn't identify anybody. We didn't have the photo in our gallery. Why should anybody guess she wouldn't be safe?"

"You cops let her die!" Crane cried. "The gunman must have had a police record elsewhere. He was afraid Ellen would be shown photos from other cities. Sooner or later she would have spotted him. He couldn't let her live."

Dr. Rowland placed a hand on his shoulder. "Take it easy, son . . . Lieutenant, I can't allow this man to be excited."

Blanchard shrugged. The gesture said: *He's practically a dead man anyway, so what difference does it make?*

An ambulance interne arrived with the driver, who carried a stretcher. The interne glanced down at Crane, whistled softly, and did nothing to treat or even bandage the wound. It was too dangerous, or there was no use. The fact remained that they were taking him to die away from here.

When they transferred him to the stretcher, Crane opened his mouth to protest that he could walk under his own power. But it was less effort to let them just carry him away. Nothing was important. Ellen was dead, and so he was not afraid of death.

But there was something to be done. He wasn't sure just what it was, and lay thinking about it until cool air washed over him and he knew that he was in the street. Then he saw it.

"Wait a minute!" Crane said, lifting his head.

The stretcher stopped. The interne, holding the front end, turned his head to look down at him.

"There's not a thing that can be done for me," Crane said. "I know. I should by rights be dead. Ellen was struck no harder than I was. There must be a reason why I was kept alive. Twice I should have died and didn't—the second time when the swarthy man shot at me and nothing happened. I've been thinking, and the only answer is that I've been given time to find Ellen's murderer. That's why the swarthy man was sent my way when I was in the lunchroom, but I didn't know who he was at the time. Now I've got to find him again."

The driver said: "He's starting to rave, Doc."

"No," Crane insisted. "My brain has never been clearer. That's another miracle, for the bits of bone are pressing into my brain. And why didn't I bleed to death?"

"Lie still," the interne told him. "You can never tell about those head injuries. No two act the same way."

"Why bother kidding me?" Crane said wearily. "I've been lent time to find Ellen's murderer. It can't be any other way. So you've got to let me go."

"We'll fix you up fine in the hospital," the interne said soothingly. "Then you can go anywhere you like. Let's go, George."

As the stretcher started to move again, Crane considered making a break for it. But they would have their hands on him before he could get off the stretcher, and a struggle might be too much for him. He had to stretch his borrowed time. Perhaps when they reached the hospital they would leave him alone in the ambulance long enough for him to slip away.

They slid the stretcher into the ambulance. The driver went around to the front. The interne was about to climb inside with Crane when he paused to slap his pockets.

"Got a cigarette, George?" he called.

"You know I don't use 'em. There's a drugstore still open at the corner."

The interne sauntered off. Slowly, Crane sat up. Through the still open doors the street stretched out before him. He had told them that he wanted to escape, but they had put it down to the ravings of a badly injured man. And they were not guarding him now because they could not conceive of a man with a wound like that getting up and walking away.

Then he was standing outside the ambulance, glancing cautiously about the empty street for either the interne or the driver. He was alone.

Not quite alone. The tail of his eye caught movement in the dark doorway across the street. No more than that. No definite shape—only a stirring of deeper shadows. But he knew that it had to be the swarthy man, because he had been kept alive for only one reason. He started across the street.

The shadow moved out of the doorway and became the stocky figure of a man. He peered at Crane with his head far forward. He pulled his gun out.

Crane felt no fear. He kept going across the gutter. The swarthy man had been placed there for him by the same power that was keeping him, Crane, alive.

And the swarthy man did not shoot. With the revolver dangling forgotten from his swinging hand, he raced down the street.

Crane broke into a run. At once, nausea seized him. His head reeled; he almost fell. *Careful,* he told himself. *That's one thing you can't do.*

He walked as rapidly as he could. He followed the swarthy man around the corner, and when he saw him again, the distance between them had grown to a hundred feet. Crane ran two steps and brought himself up short before he keeled over. He could not run without jerking his head. A sob of helplessness tore from his throat. He kept walking, but the other was already out of sight.

After a while Crane leaned against the wall of a house to rest. He was sick now to the core of his being and his hat seemed to weigh a ton. Only he wasn't wearing a hat; it had been left in Ellen's apartment. He knew then that he hadn't much more time.

Suddenly he laughed with a bitterness that shook him. If some sort of divine Providence was keeping him alive for a certain job, then why hadn't Providence let him complete the job by catching the swarthy man? Now he had the whole city to hunt for him. That would baffle even the police, with limitless time and manpower.

But wait. There had to be a logical explanation why he had twice come across the swarthy man in the last hour. The second one was easy. The swarthy man had murdered Ellen; he had returned to the scene of the crime to learn if there were any developments which affected him.

And the first time? The swarthy man had been entering a lunchroom. He hadn't known Crane would be there. He had been shocked nearly out of his wits at the sight of the man he thought he had killed. He had merely dropped into a neighborhood lunchroom for food.

Neighborhood! The swarthy man lived somewhere near the lunchroom.

Crane did not remember walking those five blocks. It was as if his brain had blacked out, and when he came out of it he was looking at a neon sign which said: COFFEE. The weight on his head was becoming unbearable. His legs were turning to water.

Well, here he was, and except for an occasional passing car, the city slept. He moved on, slowly now, fighting to keep his thoughts from clouding and his legs from folding.

Running feet broke the silence. He stood very still, concentrating on the receding sound. And then, far down on the other side of the street, he glimpsed a fleeting shadow. Abruptly it swung away from the curb and vanished through a doorway.

It did not occur to Crane that it might not be the swarthy man he had seen. This was the completion of a pattern which had gone beyond his own logical reasoning. He did not doubt that he had been deliberately brought here for the same reason that he was still alive.

There was a fire hydrant where the shape had left the street, so he was sure of the exact spot. The hydrant was in front of a box-like two-story building. The ground floor consisted of a grocery store, and lights were in the two windows above.

There was a door to be entered, a dimly lit staircase up which to pull himself with infinite weariness, and then a small hall and another door. Men were speaking beyond that door.

One voice Crane recognized as that of the swarthy man, even though now it was shrill with terror. "I tell you, Flick, he's haunting me. Go on, laugh, but I killed that guy. I told you how he came in just when I got done with the girl, so I had to give him the business too."

"How do you know he was dead?" a bantering voice asked.

"I know how to hit 'em. It's nice and quiet and not messy. A sock on the head and they're dead before they hit the floor. And I saw what I did to that guy. Hell, half his head was knocked in!"

"Did you make sure he was dead?"

"I wasn't hanging around there longer than I had to," the swarthy man replied hesitantly. "Well, all right, say I didn't finish him. But what would he be doing hours later sitting in Steve's lunchroom, drinking coffee as calm as you please? He'd be dead or in a hospital. And he knew me, Flick. He never seen me before. How the hell did he know me? And he went after me. My gun didn't scare him none. And when I pulled the trigger, nothing happened."

"You missed him?"

"The gun was right up against him. But no bullet came out. The gun didn't shoot, and I'd just oiled and cleaned it for that payroll job."

The man named Flick chuckled derisively. "You dope! Guns miss fire lots of times."

"Maybe. So all right, the gun missed fire. So I went back to the house to see if the cops were there. They were there all right. I didn't get it. Say this guy was hurt bad, would they let him go? Then an ambulance pulls up and they carry somebody out. It's the guy, I think. Maybe I been dreaming I seen him. Then all of a sudden there he is, not in the ambulance. He's coming across the street, straight to where I'm standing. He couldn't see me. I tell you, he couldn't. I was in a doorway. But he came straight at me. So I ran."

"You're a brave lad."

"Yeah, it's funny to you. Sure I was scared. He chased after me, but the funny thing is he didn't run. He kept walking, like he knew I couldn't get away from him. But I shook him off with no trouble. I cut through yards. I went out of my way. A bloodhound couldn't have followed me." His voice faded and then rose stridently: "Listen, Flick! I'm downstairs on this street and look back —and there he is. And he's still walking, like nothing can stop him."

"You damn fool! Did he see you come in here?"

"What's the difference? He knows where we live. But how does he know? That's what I'm asking. He's supposed to be dead. I killed him."

"Of all the saps!" Flick shouted. "Maybe he's calling the cops. Go look for him."

"He don't need cops, Flick. He'll come himself. He knew all along where we lived and he didn't bring no cops."

"Then go out and get him."

"I'm scared."

"You got a gun. Use it."

There was a brief silence. Then the swarthy man said more quietly: "I get the dirty jobs. I kill the girl for you. I get sent out to kill a guy I killed once already."

"Don't be a damn fool. I'll be with you as soon as I get my pants on."

The door opened so suddenly that Crane had no time to retreat. In the dimness of the hall, he stood facing the swarthy man.

An insane moan trickled from the swarthy man's lips. He said brokenly, "Flick!" and reached under his shoulder.

Crane had no plan of action. He simply moved in, and his body struck the swarthy man and the arm which was coming out with the gun. The arm and wrist and gun-muzzle were pressed against the swarthy man at the instant the fingers contracted the trigger.

Thunder shook the small hall. The swarthy man fell away from Crane and slumped against the wall. His eyes stared sightlessly. He was dead.

"All right, guy," a voice said hoarsely. "Reach."

Crane lifted his gaze. A tall, gaunt man wearing only underwear stood in the doorway, and a black automatic was in his hand. The face was the one Ellen had described. She had died because she had seen that face during the holdup.

"So you're the lad who's been haunting Carlos." The gaunt

man's eyes flicked to the dead man and back to Crane. "How much do you know?"

Crane swayed. His knees quivered; his shoulders were bowed under the weight of his head. But he felt no fear. He felt only a little relief that he was so near the end. He said: "I know that he murdered Ellen and that you are her murderer too."

The gaunt face tightened. "What I want to know is, do the cops know?"

"They don't have to know," Crane said. His voice sounded flat and unfamiliar in his ears. "I'm going to kill you." And he moved forward.

The gun roared. Crane paused at the impact of the bullet and then resumed motion.

"Stay back!" the gaunt man gasped. "I hit you!" He retreated backward into his room. His face fell to pieces with terror.

Crane smiled. "You can't kill a dead man," he said, and lunged.

The gun spoke again as Crane's hands closed over that skinny neck. He felt nothing. He was past physical sensation.

He fell with the gaunt man under him. Once more there was the sound of a gun, distant and unimportant. Inches from his own face, Crane saw another face that no longer looked quite human. The eyes bulged, the tongue protruded, the skin turned purple.

There was no warning. Between the drawing of a breath, Jim Crane ceased to be . . .

They had a great deal of trouble loosening the dead fingers from the skinny throat of the other dead man.

Dr. Rowland, the coroner, was puzzled. "The shooting was heard only twenty minutes ago. Rigor shouldn't have set in so firmly."

Lieutenant Blanchard turned from the hall where he had been looking down at the body of the swarthy man. "Crane must have continued to hang on while he was dying from the bullet wounds."

Dr. Rowland frowned and said nothing. After a while he stood up. "Crane was hit three times, but none of the bullets could have been fatal. He was bound to drop dead any moment. The exertion of the struggle finished him."

Blanchard drew smoke deep into his lungs. "But not until he had killed these two."

"I don't understand."

"You remember what the ambulance interne told us," Blanchard said. "Crane was raving about being kept alive by something so he could avenge his sweetheart's murder. He lived just long enough to do it."

Dr. Rowland sniffed. "Nonsense! Crane wasn't the first man I've seen alive who by all laws of medical science should be dead. This is especially true where brain injuries are concerned."

"Maybe." Blanchard studied the cloud of smoke he expelled. "You're the doctor, so why should I argue?"

*A. A. Milne (1882–1956) is best known as the creator of Win-
nie-the-Pooh, but he is also fondly remembered as the author of*
The Red House Mystery *(1922), at least a minor classic, and a
handful of excellent short stories—like this wry and, I venture,
unguessable account from the 1947 anthology.*

A. A. MILNE

The Wine Glass

I am in a terrible predicament, as you will see directly. I don't
know what to do . . .

"One of the maxims which I have found most helpful in my career at Scotland Yard," the superintendent was saying, "has been
the simple one that appearances are not always deceptive. A crime
may be committed exactly as it seems to have been committed and
exactly as it was intended to be committed." He helped himself
and passed the bottle.

"I don't think I follow you," I said, hoping thus to lead him on.

I am a writer of detective stories. If you have never heard of
me, it can only be because you don't read detective stories. I
wrote "Murder on the Back Stairs" and "The Mystery of the
Twisted Eglantine," to mention only two of my successes. It
was this fact, I think, which first interested Superintendent Freder-
ick Mortimer in me, and, of course, me in him. He is a big fellow
with the face of a Roman Emperor; I am the small neat type. We
gradually became friends and so got into the habit of dining together once a month. He liked talking about his cases, and naturally I liked listening. But this evening the wine seemed to be
making itself felt.

"I don't think I follow you," I said again.

"I mean that the simple way of committing a murder is often the best way. This doesn't mean that the murderer is a man of simple mind. On the contrary. He is subtle enough to know that the simple solution is too simple to be credible."

This sounded anything but simple, so I said, "Give me an example."

"Well, take the case of the bottle of wine which was sent to the Marquis of Hedingham on his birthday. Have I never told you about it?"

"Never," I said, and I helped myself and passed the bottle.

He filled his glass and considered. "Give me a moment to get it clear," he said. "It was a long time ago." While he closed his eyes and let the past drift before him, I ordered up another bottle of the same.

"Yes," said Mortimer, opening his eyes. "I've got it now."

I leaned forward, listening eagerly. This is the story he told me.

The first we heard of it at the Yard (said Mortimer) was a brief announcement over the telephone that the Marquis of Hedingham's butler had died suddenly at His Lordship's town house in Brook Street, and that poison was suspected. This was at seven o'clock. We went around at once. Inspector Totman had been put in charge of the case; I was a young detective sergeant at the time, and I generally worked under Totman. He was a brisk, military sort of fellow, with a little prickly ginger mustache, good at his job in a showy, orthodox way, but he had no imagination, and he was thinking all the time of what Inspector Totman would get out of it. Quite frankly I didn't like him. Outwardly we kept friendly, for it doesn't do to quarrel with one's superiors; indeed, he was vain enough to think that I had a great admiration for him; but I knew that he was just using me for his own advantage, and I had a shrewd suspicion that I should have been promoted before this, if he hadn't wanted to keep me under him so that he could profit by my brains.

We found the butler in his pantry, stretched out on the floor. An open bottle of Tokay, a broken wine glass with the dregs of the liquid still in it, the medical evidence of poisoning, all helped to build up the story for us. The wine had arrived about an hour before, with the card of Sir William Kelso attached to it. On the card was a typewritten message, saying, "Bless you, Tommy, and here's something to celebrate with." I can't remember the exact words, of course, but that was the idea. Apparently it was His Lordship's birthday, and he was having a small family party of about six people for the occasion. Sir William Kelso, I should explain, was his oldest friend and a relation by marriage, Lord Hedingham having married his sister; in fact, Sir William was to have been one of the party present that evening. He was a bachelor, about fifty, and a devoted uncle to his nephew and nieces.

Well, the butler had brought up the bottle and the card to His Lordship—this was about six o'clock; and Lord Hedingham, as he told us, had taken the card, said something like, "Good old Bill. We'll have that tonight, Perkins," and Perkins had said, "Very good, My Lord," and gone out again with the bottle. The card had been left lying on the table. Afterwards there could be little doubt what had happened. Perkins had opened the bottle with the intention of decanting it but had been unable to resist the temptation to sample it first. I suspect that in his time he had sampled most of His Lordship's wine but had never before come across a Tokay of such richness. So he had poured himself out a full glass, drunk it, and died almost immediately.

"Good heavens!" I interrupted. "But how extremely providential—I mean, of course, for Lord Hedingham and the others."

"Exactly," said Mortimer, as he twirled his own wine glass. The contents of the bottle were analyzed (he went on) and found to contain a more-than-fatal dose of prussic acid. Of course we did all the routine things. With young Roberts, a nice young fellow who often worked with us, I went around to all the chemists' shops in the neighborhood. Totman examined everybody from Sir William and Lord Hedingham downwards.

Roberts and I took the bottle round to all the wine merchants in the neighborhood. At the end of a week all we could say was this:

One: The murderer had a motive for murdering Lord Hedingham; or, possibly, somebody at his party; or, possibly, the whole party. In accordance with the usual custom, His Lordship would be the first to taste the wine. A sip would not be fatal, and in a wine of such richness the taste might not be noticeable; so that the whole party would then presumably drink His Lordship's health. He would raise his glass to them, and in this way they would all take the poison, and be affected according to how deeply they drank. On the other hand, His Lordship might take a good deal more than a sip in the first place, and so be the only one to suffer. My deduction from this was that the motive was revenge rather than gain. The criminal would avenge himself on Lord Hedingham if His Lordship or any of his family were seriously poisoned; he could only profit if definite people were definitely killed. It took a little time to get Totman to see this, but he did eventually agree.

Two: The murderer had been able to obtain one of Sir William Kelso's cards, and knew that John Richard Mervyn Plantaganet Carlow, tenth Marquis of Hedingham, was called "Tommy" by his intimates. Totman deduced from this that he was therefore one of the Hedingham-Kelso circle of relations and friends. I disputed this. I pointed out: (a) that it was to strangers rather than to intimate friends that cards were presented, except in the case of formal calls, when they were left in a bowl or tray in the hall, and anybody could steal one; (b) that the fact that Lord Hedingham was called Tommy must have appeared in society papers and be known to many people; and, most convincing of all, (c) that the murderer did not know that Sir William Kelso was to be in the party that night. For obviously some reference would have been made to the gift, either on his arrival or when the wine was served; whereupon he would have disclaimed any knowledge of it, and the bottle would immediately have been suspected. As it was, of course, Perkins had drunk from it before Sir William's arrival. Now both Sir William and Lord Hedingham assured us that they *always* dined together on each other's birthday, and they were convinced that any personal friend of theirs would have been aware of the fact. I made Totman question them about this, and he then came round to my opinion.

Three: There was nothing to prove that the wine in the bottle corresponded to the label; and wine experts were naturally reluctant to taste it for us. All they could say from the smell was that it was a Tokay of sorts. This, of course, made it more difficult for us. In fact I may say that neither from the purchase of the wine nor the nature of the poison did we get any clue.

We had, then, the following picture of the murderer. He had a cause of grievance, legitimate or fancied, against Lord Hedingham, and did not scruple to take the most terrible revenge. He knew that Sir William Kelso was a friend of His Lordship and called him Tommy, and that he might reasonably give him a bottle of wine on his birthday. He did *not* know that Sir William would be dining there that night; that is to say, *even as late as six o'clock that evening,* he did not know. He was not likely, therefore, to be anyone at present employed or living in Lord Hedingham's house. Finally, he had had an opportunity to get hold of a card of Sir William's.

As it happened, there was somebody who fitted completely into this picture. It was a fellow called—wait a bit—Merrivale, Medley—oh, well, it doesn't matter. Merton, that was it. Merton. He had been His Lordship's valet for six months, had been suspected of stealing and had been dismissed without a character reference. Just the man we wanted. So for a fortnight we searched for Merton. And then, when at last we got on to him, we discovered that he had the most complete alibi imaginable. (*The superintendent held up his hand, and it came into my mind that he must have stopped the traffic as a young man with just that gesture.*) Yes, I know what you're going to say, what you detective-story writers always say—the better an alibi, the worse it is. Well, sometimes, I admit; but not in this case. For Merton was in jail, under another name, and he had been inside for the last two months. And what do you think he was suspected of, and was waiting trial for? Oh, well, of course you guess; I've as good as told you. He was on a charge of murder—and murder, mark you, by poison.

"Good heavens!" I interjected. I seized the opportunity to refill my friend's glass. He said, "Exactly," and took a long drink.

You can imagine (he went on) what a shock this was to us. You see, a certain sort of murder had been committed; we had deduced that it was done by a certain man, without knowing whether he was in the least capable of such a crime; and now, having proved to the hilt that he *was* capable of it, we had simultaneously proved that he didn't do it.

I said to Totman, "Let's take a couple of days off, and each of us think it out, then pool our ideas and start afresh."

Totman frisked up his little mustache and laughed in his conceited way. "You don't think I'm going to admit myself wrong, do you, when I've just proved I'm right?" (Totman saying "I," when he had got everything from me!) "Merton's my man. He'd got the bottle ready, and somebody else delivered it for him. That's all.

He had to wait for the birthday, you see, and when he found himself in prison, his wife or somebody—"

"—took round the bottle, all nicely labeled 'Poison; not to be
delivered till Christmas Day.' " I had to say it, I was so annoyed
with him.

"Don't be more of a damned fool than you can help," he
shouted, "and don't be insolent, or you'll get into trouble."

I apologized humbly and told him how much I liked working
with him. He forgave me, and we were friends again. He patted
me on the shoulder.

"You take a day off," he said kindly, "you've been working too
hard. Take a bus into the country and make up a good story for
me; the story of that bottle, and how it came from Merton's lodg-
ing to Brook Street, and who took it and why. I admit I don't see
it at present, but that's the bottle, you can bet your life. I'm going
down to Leatherhead. Report here on Friday morning, and we'll
see what we've got. My birthday as it happens, and I feel I'm
going to be lucky." Leatherhead was where an old woman had
been poisoned. That was the third time in a week he'd told me
when his wretched birthday was.

I took a bus to Hampstead Heath. I walked round the Leg of
Mutton Pond twenty times. And each time that I went round, Totman's theory seemed sillier than the last time. And each time I
felt more and more strongly that we were being *forced* into an entirely artificial interpretation of things. It sounds fantastic, I know,
but I could almost feel the murderer behind us, pushing us along
the way he wanted us to go.

I sat down on a seat and filled a pipe, and I said, "Right! The
murderer's a man who wanted me to believe all that I have believed. When I've told myself that the murderer intended to do
so-and-so, he intended me to believe that, and therefore he didn't
do so-and-so. When I've told myself that the murderer wanted to
mislead me, he wanted me to think he wanted to mislead me,
which meant that the truth was exactly as it seemed to be. Now
then, Fred, you'll begin all over again, and you'll take things as
they are and won't be too clever about them. Because the murderer expects you to be clever, and wants you to be clever, and
from now on you aren't going to take your orders from *him*."

And of course, the first thing which leaped to my mind was that
the murderer *meant* to murder the butler!

It seemed incredible now that we could ever have missed it. Didn't every butler sample his master's wines? Why, it was an absolute certainty that Perkins would be the first victim of a poisoned bottle of a very special vintage. What butler could resist pouring himself out a glass as he decanted it?

Wait, though. Mustn't be in a hurry. Two objections. One: Perkins might be the one butler in a thousand who wasn't a wine-sampler. Two: Even if he were like any other butler, he might be out of sorts on that particular evening and have put by a glass to drink later. Wouldn't it be much too risky for a murderer who only wanted to destroy Perkins, and had no grudge against Lord Hedingham's family, to depend so absolutely on the butler drinking first?

For a little while this held me up, but not for long. Suddenly I saw the complete solution.

It would *not* be risky if (a) the murderer had certain knowledge of the butler's habits; and (b) could, if necessary, at the last moment, prevent the family from drinking. In other words, if he were an intimate of the family, were himself present at the party, and, without bringing suspicion on himself, could bring the wine under suspicion.

In other words, only if he were Sir William Kelso! For Sir William was the only man in the world who could say, "Don't drink this wine. I'm supposed to have sent it to you, and I didn't, so that proves it's a fake." The *only* man.

Why hadn't we suspected him from the beginning? One reason, of course, was that we had supposed the intended victim to be one of the Hedingham family, and of Sir William's devotion to his sister, brother-in-law, nephew and nieces, there was never any doubt. But the chief reason was our assumption that the last thing a murderer would do would be to give himself away by sending his own card round with the poisoned bottle. "The *last* thing a murderer would do"—and therefore the *first* thing a really clever murderer would do.

To make my case complete to myself, for I had little hope as yet of converting Totman, I had to establish motive. Why should Sir William want to murder Perkins? I gave myself the pleasure of having tea that afternoon with Lord Hedingham's housekeeper. We had caught each other's eye on other occasions when I had been at the house, and—well, I suppose I can say it now—I had a way with the women in those days. When I left, I knew two things. Perkins had been generally unpopular, not only downstairs, but upstairs. "It was a wonder how they put up with him." And Her Ladyship had been "a different woman lately."

"How different?" I asked.

"So much younger, if you know what I mean, Sergeant Mortimer. Almost like a girl again, bless her heart."

I did know. And that was that. Blackmail.

What was I do to? What did my evidence amount to? Nothing. It was all corroborative evidence. If Kelso had done one suspicious thing, or left one real clue, then the story I had made up would have convinced any jury. As it was, in the eyes of a jury he had done one completely unsuspicious thing and had left one real clue to his innocence—his visiting card. Totman would just laugh at me.

I disliked the thought of being laughed at by Totman. I wondered how I could get the laugh on him. I took a bus to Baker Street, and walked into Regent's Park, not minding where I was going, but just thinking. And then, as I got opposite Hanover Terrace, who should I see but young Roberts.

"Hallo, young fellow, what have *you* been up to?"

"Hallo, Sarge," he grinned. "Been calling on my old school chum, Sir William Kelso—or rather, his valet. Tottie thought he might have known Merton. Speaking as one valet to another, so to speak."

"Is Inspector Totman back?" I asked.

Roberts stood to attention, and said, "No Sergeant Mortimer, Inspector Totman is not expected to return from Leatherhead, Surrey, until a late hour tonight."

You couldn't be angry with the boy. At least I couldn't. He had no respect for anybody, but he was a good lad. And he had an eye like a hawk. Saw everything and forgot none of it.

I said, "I didn't know Sir William lived up this way."

Roberts pointed across the road. "Observe the august mansion. Five minutes ago you'd have found me in the basement, talking to a housemaid who thought Merton was a town in Surrey. As it is, of course."

I had a sudden crazy idea.

"Well, now you're going back there," I said. "I'm going to call on Sir William, and I want you handy. Would they let you in at the basement again, or are they sick of you?"

"Sarge, they just love me. When I went, they said, 'Must you go?' "

We say at the Yard, "Once a murderer, always a murderer." Perhaps that was why I had an absurd feeling that I should like young Roberts within call. Because I was going to tell Sir William Kelso what I'd been thinking about by the Leg of Mutton Pond. I'd only seen him once, but he gave me the idea of being the sort of man who wouldn't mind killing, but didn't like lying. I thought he would give himself away . . . and then—well, there might be a roughhouse, and Roberts would be useful.

As we walked in at the gate together, I looked in my pocket-book for a card. Luckily I had one left, though it wasn't very clean. It was a bit ink-stained, in fact. Roberts, who never missed anything said, "Personally I always use blotting paper," and went on whistling. If I hadn't known him, I shouldn't have known what he was talking about. I said, "Oh, do you?" and rang the bell. I gave the maid my card and asked if Sir William could see me, and at the same time Roberts gave her a wink and indicated the back door. She nodded to him, and asked me to come in. Roberts went down and waited for her in the basement. I felt safer.

Sir William was a big man, as big as I was. But of course a lot older. He said, "Well, Sergeant, what can I do for you?" twiddling my card in his fingers. He seemed quite friendly about it. "Sit down, won't you?"

I said, "I think I'll stand, Sir William. I want just to ask you one question, if I may?" Yes, I know I was crazy, but somehow I felt inspired.

"By all means," he said, obviously not much interested.

"When did you first discover that Perkins was blackmailing Lady Hedingham?"

He was standing in front of his big desk, and I was opposite him. He stopped fiddling with my card and became absolutely still; and there was a silence so complete that I could feel it in every nerve of my body. I kept my eyes on his, you may be sure. We stood there, I don't know how long.

"Is that the only question?" he asked. The thing that frightened me was that his voice was just the same as before. Ordinary.

"Well, just one more. Have you a typewriter in your house?" Just corroborative evidence again, that's all. But it told him that I knew.

He gave a long sigh, tossed the card into the wastepaper basket and walked to the window. He stood there with his back to me, looking out but seeing nothing. Thinking. He must have stood there for a couple of minutes. Then he turned around, and to my amazement he had a friendly smile on his face. "I think we'd both better sit down," he said. We did.

"There is a typewriter in the house which I sometimes use," he began. "I daresay you use one too."

"I do."

"And so do thousands of other people—including, it may be, the murderer you are looking for."

"Thousands of people, including the murderer," I agreed.

He noticed the difference, and smiled. "People" I had said not "other people." And I didn't say I was looking for him. Because I had found him.

"And then," I went on, "there was the actual wording of the typed message."

"Was there anything remarkable about it?"

"No. Except that it was exactly right."

"Oh, my dear fellow, anyone could have got it right. A simple birthday greeting."

"Anyone in your own class, Sir William, who knew you both. But that's all. It's Inspector Totman's birthday tomorrow." I added to myself: As he keeps telling us, damn him!

"If I sent him a bottle of whiskey, young Roberts—that's the constable who's in on this case; you may have seen him about, he's waiting for me now down below"—I thought this was rather a neat way of getting that in—"Roberts could make a guess at what I'd say, and so could anybody at the Yard who knows us both, and they wouldn't be far wrong. But you couldn't, Sir William."

He looked at me. He couldn't take his eyes off me. I wondered what he was thinking. At last he said, "You'd probably say, 'A long life and all the best, with the admiring good wishes of—' How's that?"

It was devilish. First that he had really been thinking it out when he had so much else to think about, and then that he'd got it so right. That "admiring" which meant that he'd studied Totman just as he was studying me, and knew how I'd play up to him.

"You see," he smiled, "it isn't really difficult. And the fact that my card was used is in itself convincing evidence of my innocence, don't you think?"

"To a jury perhaps," I said, "but not to me."

"I wish I could convince *you*," he murmured to himself. "Well, what are you doing about it?"

"I shall, of course, put my reconstruction of the case in front of Inspector Totman tomorrow."

"Ah! A nice birthday surprise for him. And, knowing your Totman, what do you think he will do?"

He had me there, and he knew it.

"I think *you* know him too, Sir," I said.

"I do," he smiled.

"And me, I daresay, and anybody else you meet. Quick as lightning. But even ordinary men like me have a sort of sudden understanding of people sometimes. As I've got of you, Sir. And I've a sort of feeling that, if ever we get you into a witness box, and you've taken the oath, you won't find perjury so much to your liking as murder. Or what the law calls murder."

"But *you* don't?" he said quickly.

"I think," I said, "that there are a lot of people who *ought* to be killed. But I'm a policeman, and what I think isn't evidence. You killed Perkins, didn't you?"

He nodded; and then said almost with a grin at me, "A nervous affection of the head, if you put it in evidence. I could get a specialist to swear to it."

My God, he was a good sort of man. I was really sorry when they found him next day, after he'd put a bullet through his head. And yet what else could he do? He knew I should get him.

I was furious with Fred Mortimer. That was no way to end a story. Suddenly, like that, as if he were tired of it. I told him so.

"My dear little friend," he said, "it isn't the end. We're just coming to the exciting part. This will make your hair curl."

"Oh!" I said sarcastically. "Then I suppose all that you've told me so far is just introduction?"

"That's right. Now you listen. On Friday morning, before we heard of Sir William's death, I went in to report to Inspector Totman. He wasn't there. Nobody knew where he was. They rang up his apartment house. Now hold tight to the leg of the table or something. When the porter got into his flat, he found Totman's body. Poisoned."

"Good heavens!" I ejaculated.

"You may say so. There he was, and on the table was a newly opened bottle of whiskey, and by the side of it a visiting card. And whose card do you think it was? *Mine!* And what do you think it said? 'A long life and all the best, with the admiring good wishes of—' *me!* Lucky for me I had had young Roberts with me. Lucky for me he had this genius for noticing and remembering. Lucky for me he could swear to the exact shape of the smudge of ink on that card. And I might add, lucky for me that they believed me when I told them word for word what had been said at my interview with Sir William, as I have just told you. I was reprimanded, of course, for exceeding my duty, as I most certainly had, but that was only official. Unofficially, they were very pleased with me. We couldn't prove anything, naturally, and Sir William's suicide was left unexplained. But a month later I was promoted to Inspector."

Mortimer fixed his glass and drank, while I revolved his extraordinary story in my mind.

"The theory," I said, polishing my glasses thoughtfully, "was, I suppose, that Sir William sent the poisoned whiskey, not so much to get rid of Totman, from whom he had little to fear, as to discredit you by bringing you under suspicion, and to discredit entirely your own theory of the other murder."

"Exactly."

"And then, at the last moment he realized that he couldn't go on with it, or the weight of his crimes became suddenly too much for him, or—"

"Something of the sort. Nobody ever knew, of course."

I looked across the table with sudden excitement; almost with awe.

"Do you remember what he said to you?" I asked, giving the words their full meaning as I slowly quoted them. " 'The fact that my card was used is in itself convincing evidence of my innocence . . .' And you said, 'Not to me.' And he said, 'I wish I could convince *you.*' *And that was how he did it!* The fact that your card was used was convincing evidence of your innocence!"

"With the other things. The proof that he was in possession of the particular card of mine which was used, and the certainty that he had committed the other murder. Once a poisoner, always a poisoner."

"True . . . yes . . . Well, thanks very much for the story, Fred. All the same, you know," I said, shaking my head at him, "it doesn't altogether prove what you set out to prove."

"What was that?"

"That the simple explanation is generally the true one. In the case of Perkins, yes. But not in the case of Totman."

"Sorry, I don't follow."

"My dear fellow," I said, putting up a finger to emphasize my point, for he seemed a little hazy with the wine suddenly; "the simple explanation of Totman's death—surely?—would have been that *you* had sent him the poisoned whiskey."

Superintendent Mortimer looked a little surprised. "But I did," he said.

So now you see my terrible predicament. I could hardly listen as he went on dreamily: "I never liked Totman, and he stood in my way; but I hadn't seriously thought of getting rid of him until I got that card into my hands again. As I told you, Sir William dropped it into the basket and turned to the window, and I thought; Damn it, *you* can afford to chuck about visiting cards, but I can't. It's the only one I've got left, and if you don't want it, I do. So I bent down very naturally to tie my shoelace and felt in the basket behind me, because, of course, it was rather an undignified thing to do, and I didn't want to be seen; and just as I was putting it into my pocket I saw that ink smudge again, and I remembered that Roberts had seen it. And in a flash the whole plan came to me; simple; foolproof. And from that moment everything I said to him was in preparation for it. Of course we were quite alone, but you never knew who might be listening, and besides" —he twiddled the stem of his wine glass—"p'raps I'm like Sir William, rather tell the truth than not. And it was true, all of it— how Sir William came to know about Totman's birthday, and knew that those were the very words I should have used.

"Don't think I wanted to put anything on to Sir William that wasn't his. I liked him. But he as good as told me he wasn't going to wait for what was coming to him, and he'd done one murder anyway. That was why I slipped down with a bottle that evening and left it outside Totman's flat. Didn't dare wait till the morning, in case Sir William closed his account that night." He stood up and stretched himself. "Ah, well, it was a long time ago. Good-by, old man, I must be off. Thanks for a grand dinner. Don't forget, you're dining with *me* next Tuesday. I've got a new Burgundy for you. You'll like it."

He drained his wine glass and swaggered out, leaving me to my thoughts.

From the 1948 anthology . . .

*The Checklist found at the end of this volume reveals that El-
lery Queen is the author with the most selections, appearing in
eleven of the twenty-five volumes. The same Checklist also records
that more of the 334 stories came originally from* Ellery Queen's
Mystery Magazine *than from any other single source. This illus-
trates, however inadequately, the immense contributions made by
Queen to the crime short story, both as writer and editor. . . .
The present exercise in the deductive skills of Queen the detective
is without crime, but notable in its effective embrace of history
and the neatness of its puzzle.*

ELLERY QUEEN

*The Adventure of the President's
Half Disme*

Those few curious men who have chosen to turn off the humdrum
highway to hunt for their pleasure along the back trails expect—
indeed, they look confidently forward to—many strange encounters; and it is the dull stalk which does not turn up at least a hip-
pograff. But it remained for Ellery Queen to experience the
ultimate excitement. On one of his prowls he collided with a President of the United States.

This would have been joy enough if it had occurred as you
might imagine; by chance, on a dark night, in some back street of
Washington, D.C., with Secret Service men closing in on the delighted Mr. Queen to question his motives by way of his pockets
while a large black bullet-proof limousine rushed up to spirit the
President away. But mere imagination fails in this instance. What

is required is the power of fancy, for the truth is fantastic. Ellery's encounter with the President of the United States took place, not on a dark night, but in the unromantic light of several days (although the night played its role, too). Nor was it by chance: the meeting was arranged by a farmer's daughter. And it was not in Washington, D.C., for this President presided over the affairs of the nation from a different city altogether. Not that the meeting took place in that city, either; it did not take place in a city at all, but on a farm some miles south of Philadelphia. Oddest of all, there was no limousine to spirit the Chief Executive away, for while the President was a man of great wealth, he was still too poor to possess an automobile and, what is more, not all the resources of his Government—indeed, not all the riches of the world—could have provided one for him.

There are even more curious facets to this jewel of paradox. This was an encounter in the purest sense, and yet, physically, it did not occur at all. The President in question was dead. And while there are those who would not blink at a nubbing of shoulders or a clasping of hands even though one of the parties was in his grave, and to such persons the thought might occur that the meeting took place on a psychic plane—alas, Ellery Queen is not of their company. He does not believe in ghosts, consequently he never encounters them. So he did not collide with the President's shade, either.

And yet their meeting was as palpable as, say, the meeting between two chess masters, one in Moscow and the other in New York, who never leave their respective armchairs and still play a game to a decision. It is even more wonderful than that, for while the chess players merely annihilate space, Ellery and the father of his country annihilated time—a century and a half of it.

In fine, this is the story of how Ellery Queen matched wits with George Washington.

Those who are finicky about their fashions complain that the arms of coincidence are too long; but in this case the Designer might say that He cut to measure. Or, to put it another way, an event often brews its own mood. Whatever the cause—whether coincidental or incidental—the fact is The Adventure of the President's Half Disme, which was to concern itself with the events surrounding President Washington's fifty-ninth birthday, actually first engrossed Ellery on February the nineteenth and culminated three days later.

Ellery was in his study that morning of the nineteenth of February, wrestling with several reluctant victims of violence, none of them quite flesh and blood, since his novel was still in the planning stage. So he was annoyed when Nikki came in with a card.

"James Ezekiel Patch," growled the great man; he was never in his best humor during the planning state. "I don't know any James Ezekiel Patch, Nikki. Toss the fellow out and get back to transcribing those notes on Possible Motives—"

"Why, Ellery," said Nikki. "This isn't like you at all."

"What isn't like me?"

"To renege on an appointment."

"Appointment? Does this Patch character claim—?"

"He doesn't merely claim it. He proves it."

"Someone's balmy," snarled Mr. Queen; and he strode into the living room to contend with James Ezekiel Patch. This, he perceived as soon as James Ezekiel Patch rose from the Queen fireside chair, was likely to be a heroic project. Mr. Patch, notwithstanding his mild, even studious, eyes, seemed to rise indefinitely; he was a large, a very large, man.

"Now what's all this, what's all this?" demanded Ellery fiercely; for after all Nikki was there.

"That's what I'd like to know," said the large man amiably. "What did you want with me, Mr. Queen?"

"What did I want with you! What did you want with me?"

"I find this very strange, Mr. Queen."

"Now see here, Mr. Patch, I happen to be extremely busy this morning—"

"So am I." Mr. Patch's large thick neck was reddening and his tone was no longer amiable. Ellery took a cautious step backward as his visitor lumbered forward to thrust a slip of yellow paper under his nose. "Did you send me this wire, or didn't you?"

Ellery considered it tactically expedient to take the telegram, although for strategic reasons he did so with a bellicose scowl.

IMPERATIVE YOU CALL AT MY HOME TOMORROW FEBRUARY NINETEEN PROMPTLY TEN A.M. SIGNED ELLERY QUEEN

"Well, sir?" thundered Mr. Patch. "Do you have something on Washington for me, or don't you?"

"Washington?" said Ellery absently, studying the telegram.

"George Washington, Mr. Queen! I'm Patch the antiquarian. I *collect* Washington. I'm an *authority* on Washington. I have a large fortune and I spend it all on Washington! I'd never have wasted my time this morning if your name hadn't been signed to this wire! This is my busiest week of the year. I have engagements to speak on Washington—"

"Desist, Mr. Patch," said Ellery. "This is either a practical joke, or—"

"The Baroness Tchek," announced Nikki clearly. "With another telegram." And then she added: "And Professor John Cecil Shaw, ditto."

The three telegrams were identical.

"Of course, I didn't send them," said Ellery thoughtfully, regarding his three visitors. Baroness Tchek was a short powerful woman, resembling a dumpling with gray hair; an angry dumpling. Professor Shaw was lank and long-jawed, wearing a sack suit which hung in some places and failed in its purpose by inches at the extremities. Along with Mr. Patch, they constituted as deliciously queer a trio as had ever congregated in the Queen apartment. Their host suddenly determined not to let go of them. "On the other hand, someone obviously did, using my name . . ."

"Then there's nothing more to be said," snapped the Baroness, snapping her bag for emphasis.

"I should think there's a great deal more to be said," began Professor Shaw in a troubled way. "Wasting people's time this way—"

"It's not going to waste any more of *my* time," growled the large Mr. Patch. "Washington's Birthday only three days off—!"

"Exactly," smiled Ellery. "Won't you all sit down? There's more in this than meets the eye . . . Baroness Tchek, if I'm not mistaken, you're the one who brought that fabulous collection of rare coins into the United States just before Hitler invaded Czechoslovakia? You're in the rare-coin business in New York now?"

"Unfortunately," said the Baroness coldly, "one must eat."

"And you sir? I seem to know you."

"Rare books," said the Professor in the same troubled way.

"Of course. John Cecil Shaw, the rare-book collector. We've met at Mim's and other places. I abandon my first theory. There's a pattern here, distinctly unhumorous. An antiquarian, a coin dealer, and a collector of rare books—Nikki? Whom have you out there this time?"

"If this one collects anything," muttered Nikki into her employer's ear, "I'll bet it's things with two legs and hair on their chests. A darned pretty girl—"

"Named Martha Clarke," said a cool voice; and Ellery turned to find himself regarding one of the most satisfying sights in the world.

"Ah. I take it, Miss Clarke, you also received one of these wires signed with my name?"

"Oh, no," said the pretty girl. "I'm the one who sent them."

There was something about the comely Miss Clarke which inspired, if not confidence, at least an openness of mind. Perhaps it was the self-possessed manner in which she sat all of them, including Ellery, down in Ellery's living room while she waited on the hearth-rug, like a conductor on the podium, for them to settle in their chairs. And it was the measure of Miss Clarke's assurance that none of them was indignant, only curious.

"I'll make it snappy," said Martha Clarke briskly. "I did what I did the way I did it because, first, I had to make sure I could see Mr. Patch, Baroness Tchek and Professor Shaw today. Second, because I may need a detective before I'm through . . . Third," she added, almost absently, "because I'm pretty desperate.

"My name is Martha Clarke. My father Tobias is a farmer. Our farm lies just south of Philadelphia, it was built by a Clarke in 1761, and it's been in our family ever since. I won't go gooey on you. We're broke and there's a mortgage. Unless papa and I can raise six thousand dollars in the next couple of weeks we lose the old homestead."

Professor Shaw looked vague. But the Baroness said: "Deplorable, Miss Clarke. Now if I'm to run my auction this afternoon—"

And James Ezekiel Patch grumbled: "If it's money you want, young woman—"

"Certainly it's money I want. But I have something to sell."

"Ah!" said the Baroness.

"Oh?" said the Professor.

"Hm," said the antiquarian.

Mr. Queen said nothing, and Miss Porter jealously chewed the end of her pencil.

"The other day, while I was cleaning out the attic, I found an old book."

"Well, now," said Professor Shaw indulgently. "An old book, eh?"

"It's called *The Diary of Simeon Clarke*. Simeon Clarke was papa's great-great-great-something or other. His *Diary* was privately printed in 1792 in Philadelphia, Professor, by a second cousin of his, Jonathan, who was in the printing business there."

"Jonathan Clarke. *The Diary of Simeon Clarke,*" mumbled the cadaverous book collector. "I don't believe I know either, Miss Clarke. Have you . . . ?"

Martha Clarke carefully unclasped a large manila envelope and drew forth a single yellowed sheet of badly printed paper.

"The title page was loose, so I brought it along."

Professor Shaw silently examined Miss Clarke's exhibit, and Ellery got up to squint at it. "Of course," said the Professor after a long scrutiny, in which he held the sheet up to the light, peered apparently at individual characters, and performed other mysterious rites, "mere age doesn't connote rarity, nor does rarity of itself constitute value. And while this page looks genuine for the purported period and is rare enough to be unknown to me, still . . ."

"Suppose I told you" said Miss Martha Clarke, "that the chief purpose of the *Diary*—which I have at home—is to tell the story of how George Washington visited Simeon Clarke's farm in the winter of 1791—"

"Clarke's farm? 1791?" exclaimed James Ezekiel Patch. "Preposterous. There's no record of—"

"And of what George Washington buried there," the farmer's daughter concluded.

By executive order, the Queen telephone was taken off its hook, the door was bolted, the shades were drawn, and the long interrogation began. By the middle of the afternoon, the unknown chapter in the life of the Father of His Country was fairly sketched.

Early on an icy gray February morning in 1791, Farmer Clarke had looked up from the fence he was mending to observe a splendid cortège galloping down on him from the direction of the City of Philadelphia. Outriders thundered in the van, followed by a considerable company of gentlemen on horseback and several great coaches-and-six driven by liveried Negroes. To Simeon Clarke's astonishment, the entire equipage stopped before his farmhouse. He began to run. He could hear the creak of springs and the snorting of sleek and sweating horses. Gentlemen and lackeys were leaping to the frozen ground and, by the time Simeon had reached the farmhouse, all were elbowing about the first coach, a magnificent affair bearing a coat of arms. Craning, the farmer saw within the coach a very large, great-nosed gentlemen clad in a black velvet suit and a black cloak faced with gold; there was a cocked hat on his wigged head and a great sword in a white leather scabbard at his side. This personage was on one knee, leaning with an expression of considerable anxiety over a chubby lady of middle age, swathed in furs, who was half-sitting, half-lying on the upholstered seat, her eyes closed and her cheeks waxen under the rouge. Another gentleman, soberly attired, was stooping over the lady, his fingers on one pale wrist.

"I fear," he was saying with great gravity to the kneeling man, "that it would be imprudent to proceed another yard in this weather, Your Excellency. Lady Washington requires physicking and a warm bed immediately."

Lady Washington! Then the large, richly dressed gentleman was the President! Simeon Clarke pushed excitedly through the throng.

"Your Mightiness! Sir!" he cried. "I am Simeon Clarke. This is my farm. We have warm beds, Sarah and I!"

The President considered Simeon briefly. "I thank you, Farmer Clarke. No, no, Dr. Craik. I shall assist Lady Washington myself."

And George Washington carried Martha Washington into the little Pennsylvania farmhouse of Simeon and Sarah Clarke. An aide informed the Clarkes that President Washington had been on his way to Virginia to celebrate his fifty-ninth birthday in the privacy of Mount Vernon.

Instead, he passed his birthday on the Clarke farm, for the physician insisted that the President's lady could not be moved even back to the nearby Capital, without risking complications. On His Excellency's order, the entire incident was kept secret. "It would give needless alarm to the people," he said. But he did not leave Martha's bedside for three days and three nights.

Presumably during those seventy-two hours, while his lady recovered from her indisposition, the President devoted some thought to his hosts, for on the fourth morning he sent black Christopher, his body servant, to summon the Clarkes. They found George Washington by the kitchen fire, shaven and powdered and in immaculate dress, his stern features composed.

"I am told, Farmer Clarke, that you and your good wife refuse reimbursement for the live stock you have slaughtered in the accommodation of our large company."

"You're my President, Sir," said Simeon. "I wouldn't take money."

"We—we wouldn't take money, Your Worship," stammered Sarah.

"Nonetheless, Lady Washington and I would acknowledge your hospitality in some kind. If you give me leave, I shall plant with my own hands a grove of oak saplings behind your house. And beneath one of the saplings I propose to bury two of my personal possessions." Washington's eyes twinkled ever so slightly. "It is my birthday—I feel a venturesome spirit. Come, Farmer Clarke and Mistress Clarke, would you like that?"

"What—what were they?" choked James Ezekiel Patch, the Washington collector. He was pale.

Martha Clarke replied: "The sword at Washington's side, in its white leather scabbard, and a silver coin the President carried in a secret pocket."

"Silver *coin?*" breathed Baroness Tchek, the rare-coin dealer. "What kind of coin, Miss Clarke?"

"The *Diary* calls it 'a half disme,' with an *s,*" replied Martha Clarke, frowning. "I guess that's the way they spelled dime in those days. The book's full of queer spellings."

"A United States of America half disme?" asked the Baroness in a very odd way.

"That's what it says, Baroness."

"And this was in February, 1791?"

"Yes."

The Baroness snorted, beginning to rise. "I thought your story was too impossibly romantic, young woman. The United States Mint didn't begin to strike off half dismes until 1792!"

"Half dismes or any other U. S. coinage, I believe," said Ellery. "How come, Miss Clarke?"

"It was an experimental coin," said Miss Clarke coolly. "The *Diary* isn't clear as to whether it was the Mint which struck it off, or some private agency—maybe Washington himself didn't tell Simeon—but the President did say to Simeon that the half disme in his pocket had been coined from silver he himself had furnished and had been presented to him as a keepsake."

"There's a half disme with a story like that behind it in the possession of The American Numismatic Society," muttered the Baroness, "but it's definitely called one of the earliest coins struck off by the Mint. It's possible, I suppose, that in 1791, the preceding year, some specimen coins may have been struck off—"

"Possible my foot," said Miss Clarke. "It's so. The *Diary* says so. I imagine President Washington was pretty interested in the coins to be issued by the new country he was head of."

"Miss Clarke, I—I want that half disme. I mean—I'd like to buy it from you," said the Baroness.

"And I," said Mr. Patch carefully, "would like to ah . . . purchase Washington's sword."

"The *Diary,*" moaned Professor Shaw. "I'll buy *The Diary of Simeon Clarke* from you, Miss Clarke!"

"I'll be happy to sell it to you, Professor Shaw—as I said, I found it in the attic and I have it locked up in a highboy in the parlor at home. But as for the other two things . . ." Martha Clarke paused, and Ellery looked delighted. He thought he knew what was coming. "I'll sell you the sword, Mr. Patch, and you the half disme, Baroness Tchek, providing—" and now Miss Clarke turned her clear eyes on Ellery "—providing you, Mr. Queen, will be kind enough to find them."

And there was the farmhouse in the frosty Pennsylvania morning, set in the barren winter acres, and looking as bleak as only a little Revolutionary house with a mortgage on its head can look in the month of February.

"There's an apple orchard over there," said Nikki as they got out of Ellery's car. "But where's the grove of oaks? I don't see any!" And then she added, sweetly: "Do you, Ellery?"

Ellery's lips tightened. They tightened further when his solo on the front-door knocker brought no response.

"Let's go around," he said briefly; and Nikki preceded him with cheerful step.

Behind the house there was a barn; and beyond the barn there was comfort, at least for Ellery. For beyond the barn there were twelve ugly holes in the earth, and beside each hole lay either a freshly felled oak tree and its stump, or an ancient stump by itself, freshly uprooted. On one of the stumps sat an old man in earth-stained blue jeans, smoking a corncob pugnaciously.

"Tobias Clarke?" asked Ellery.

"Yump."

"I'm Ellery Queen. This is Miss Porter. Your daughter visited me in New York yesterday—"

"Know all about it."

"May I ask where Martha is?"

"Station. Meetin' them there other folks." Tobias Clarke spat and looked away—at the holes. "Don't know what ye're all comin' down here for. Wasn't nothin' under them oaks. Dug 'em all up t'other day. Trees that were standin' and the stumps of the ones that'd fallen years back. Look at them holes. Hired hand and me dug down most to China. Washin'ton's Grove, always been called. Now look at it. Firewood—for someone else, I guess." There was an iron bitterness in his tone. "We're losin' this farm, Mister, un-less . . ." And Tobias Clarke stopped. "Well, maybe we won't," he said. "There's always that there book Martha found."

"Professor Shaw, the rare-book collector, offered your daughter two thousand dollars for it if he's satisfied with it, Mr. Clarke," said Nikki.

"So she told me last night when she got back from New York," said Tobias Clarke. "Two thousand—and we need six." He grinned, and he spat again.

"Well," said Nikki sadly to Ellery, "that's that." She hoped Ellery would immediately get into the car and drive back to New York—immediately.

But Ellery showed no disposition to be sensible. "Perhaps, Mr. Clarke, some trees died in the course of time and just disappeared, stumps, roots, and all. Martha—" Martha! "—said the *Diary* doesn't mention the exact number Washington planted here."

"Look at them holes. Twelve of 'em, ain't there? In a triangle.

Man plants trees in a triangle, he plants trees in a triangle. Ye don't see no place between holes big enough for another tree, do ye? Anyways, there was the same distance between all the trees. No, sir, Mister, twelve was all there was ever; and I looked under all twelve."

"What's the extra tree doing in the center of the triangle? You haven't uprooted that one, Mr. Clarke."

Tobias Clarke spat once more. "Don't know much about trees, do ye? That's a cherry saplin' I set in myself six years ago. Ain't got nothin' to do with George Washin'ton."

Nikki tittered.

"If you'd sift the earth in those holes—"

"I sifted it. Look, Mister, either somebody dug that stuff up a hundred years ago or the whole yarn's a Saturday night whopper. Which it most likely is. There's Martha now with them other folks." And Tobias Clarke added, spitting for the fourth time: "Don't let me be keepin' ye."

"It reveals Washington rather er . . . out of character," said James Ezekiel Patch that evening. They were sitting about a fire in the parlor, as heavy with gloom as with Miss Clarke's dinner; and that, at least in Miss Porter's view, was heavy indeed. Baroness Tchek wore the expression of one who is trapped in a cave; there was no further train until morning, and she had not yet resigned herself to a night in a farmhouse bed. The better part of the day had been spent poring over *The Diary of Simeon Clarke,* searching for a clue to the buried Washingtonia. But there was no clue; the pertinent passage referred merely to "a Triangle of Oake Trees behinde the red Barn distant fifteen yards one from the other, which His Excellency the President did plant with his own Hands, as he had promised me, and then did burie his Sworde and the Half Disme for his Pleasure in a Case of copper beneathe one of the Oakes, the which, he said, (the Case) had been fashioned by Mr. Revere of Boston who is experimenting with this Mettle in his Furnasses."

"How out of character, Mr. Patch?" asked Ellery. He had been staring into the fire for a long time, scarcely listening.

"Washington wasn't given to romanticism," said the large man dryly. "No folderol about him. I don't know of anything in his life which prepares us for such a yarn as this. I'm beginning to think—"

"But Professor Shaw himself says the *Diary* is no forgery!" cried Martha Clarke.

"Oh, the book's authentic enough." Professor Shaw seemed unhappy. "But it may simply be a literary hoax, Miss Clarke. The woods are full of them. I'm afraid that unless the story is confirmed by the discovery of that copper case with its contents . . ."

"Oh, dear," said Nikki impulsively; and for a moment she was sorry for Martha Clarke, she really was.

But Ellery said: "I believe it. Pennsylvania farmers in 1791 weren't given to literary hoaxes, Professor Shaw. As for Washington, Mr. Patch—no man can be so rigidly consistent. And with his wife just recovering from an illness—on his own birthday . . ." And Ellery fell silent again.

Almost immediately he leaped from his chair. "Mr. Clarke!"

Tobias stirred from his dark corner. "What?"

"Did you ever hear your father, or grandfather—anyone in your family—talk of *another barn behind the house?*"

Martha stared at him. Then she cried: "Papa, that's it! It was a different barn, in a different place, and the original Washington's Grove was cut down, or died—"

"Nope," said Tobias Clarke. "Never was but this one barn. Still got some of its original timbers. Ye can see the date burned into the crosstree 1761."

Nikki was up early. A steady *hack-hack-hack* borne on frosty air woke her. She peered out of her back window, the coverlet up to her nose, to see Mr. Ellery Queen against the dawn, like a pioneer, wielding an ax powerfully.

Nikki dressed quickly, shivering, flung her mink-dyed muskrat over her shoulders, and ran downstairs, out of the house, and around it past the barn.

"Ellery! What do you think you're doing? It's practically the middle of the night!"

"Chopping," said Ellery, chopping.

"There's *mountains* of firewood stacked against the barn," said Nikki. "Really, Ellery, I think this is carrying a flirtation too far." Ellery did not reply. "And anyway, there's something—something gruesome and indecent about chopping up trees George Washington planted. It's vandalism."

"Just a thought," panted Ellery, pausing for a moment.

"A hundred and fifty-odd years is a long time, Nikki. Lots of queer things could happen, even to a tree, in that time. For instance—"

"The copper case," breathed Nikki, visibly. "The roots grew *around* it. It's *in* one of these stumps!"

"Now you're functioning," said Ellery, and he raised the ax again.

He was still at it two hours later, when Martha Clarke announced breakfast.

At 11:30 A.M. Nikki returned from driving the Professor, the Baroness, and James Ezekiel Patch to the railroad station. She found Mr. Queen seated before the fire in the kitchen in his undershirt, while Martha Clarke caressed his naked right arm.

"Oh!" said Nikki faintly. "I beg your pardon."

"Where you going, Nikki?" said Ellery irritably. "Come in. Martha's rubbing liniment into my biceps."

"He's not very accustomed to chopping wood, is he?" asked Martha Clarke in a cheerful voice.

"Reduced those foul 'oakes' to splinters," groaned Ellery. "Martha, ouch!"

"I should think you'd be satisfied now," said Nikki coldly. "I suggest we imitate Patch, Shaw, and the Baroness, Ellery—there's a 3:05. We can't impose on Miss Clarke's hospitality forever."

To Nikki's horror, Martha Clarke chose this moment to burst into tears.

"Martha!"

Nikki felt like leaping upon her and shaking the cool look back into her perfidious eyes.

"Here—here, now, Martha." That's right, thought Nikki contemptuously. Embrace her in front of me! "It's those three rats. Running out that way! Don't worry—I'll find that sword and half disme for you yet."

"You'll never find them," sobbed Martha, wetting Ellery's undershirt. "Because they're not here. They never were here. When you s-stop to think of it . . . burying that coin, his sword . . . if the story were true, he'd have given them to Simeon and Sarah . . ."

"Not necessarily, not necessarily," said Ellery with hateful haste. "The old boy had a sense of history, Martha. They all did in those days. They knew they were men of destiny and that the eyes of posterity were upon them. Burying 'em is just what Washington would have done!"

"Do you really th-think so?"

Oh . . . *pfui*.

"But even if he did bury them," Martha sniffled, "it doesn't stand to reason Simeon and Sarah would have let them *stay* buried. They'd have dug that copper box up like rabbits the minute G-George turned his back."

"Two simple countryfolk?" cried Ellery. "Salt of the earth? The new American earth? Disregard the wishes of His Mightiness, George Washington, First President of the United States? Are you out of your mind? And anyway, what would Simeon do with a dress-sword?"

Beat it into a ploughshare, thought Nikki spitefully—*that's* what he'd do.

"And that half disme. How much could it have been worth in 1791? Martha, they're here under your farm somewhere. You wait and see—"

"I wish I could b-believe it . . . Ellery."

"Shucks, child. Now stop crying—"

From the door Miss Porter said stiffly: "You might put your shirt back on, Superman, before you catch pneumonia."

Mr. Queen prowled about the Clarke acres for the remainder of that day, his nose at a low altitude. He spent some time in the barn. He devoted at least twenty minutes to each of the twelve holes in the earth. He reinspected the oaken wreckage of his ax-work, like a paleontologist examining an ancient petrifaction for the impression of a dinosaur foot. He measured off the distance between the holes; and, for a moment, a faint tremor of emotion shook him. George Washington had been a surveyor in his youth; here was evidence that his passion for exactitude had not wearied with the years. As far as Ellery could make out, the oaks had been set into the earth at exactly equal distances, in an equilateral triangle.

It was at this point that Ellery had seated himself upon the seat of a cultivator behind the barn, wondering at his suddenly accelerated circulation. Little memories were knocking at the door. And as he opened to admit them, it was as if he were admitting a personality. It was, of course, at this time that the sense of personal conflict first obtruded. He had merely to shut his eyes in order to materialize a tall, large-featured man carefully pacing off the distances between twelve points—pacing them off in a sort of objective challenge to the unborn future. George Washington . . .

The man Washington had from the beginning possessed an affinity for numbers. It had remained with him all his life. To count things, not so much for the sake of the things, perhaps, as for the counting, had been of the utmost importance to him. As a boy in Mr. Williams's school in Westmoreland, he excelled in arithmetic. Long division, subtraction, weights and measures—to calculate cords of wood and pecks of peas, pints and gallons and avoirdupois—young George delighted in these as other boys delighted in horseplay. As a man, he merely directed his passion into the channel of his possessions. Through his possessions he apparently satisfied his curious need for enumeration. He was not content simply to keep accounts of the acreage he owned, its yield, his slaves, his pounds and pence. Ellery recalled the extraordinary case of Washington and the seed. He once calculated the number of seeds in a pound Troy weight of red clover. Not appeased by the statistics on red clover, Washington then went to work on a pound of timothy seed. His conclusions were: 71,000 and 298,000. His appetite unsatisfied, he thereupon fell upon the problem of New River grass. Here he tackled a calculation worthy of his prowess: his mathematical labors produced the great, pacifying figure of 844,800.

This man was so obsessed with numbers, Ellery thought, staring at the ruins of Washington's Grove, that he counted the windows in each house of his Mount Vernon estate and the number of "Paynes" in each window of each house, and then triumphantly recorded the exact number of each in his own handwriting.

It was like a hunger, requiring periodic satiation. In 1747, as a boy of fifteen, George Washington drew "A Plan of Major Law: Washingtons Turnip Field as Survey'd by me." In 1786, at the age of fifty-four, General Washington, the most famous man in the world, occupied himself with determining the exact elevation of his piazza above the Potomac's high-water mark. No doubt he experienced a warmer satisfaction thereafter for knowing that when he sat upon his piazza looking down upon the river he was sitting exactly 124 feet 10½ inches above it.

And in 1791, as President of the United States, Ellery mused, he was striding about right here, setting saplings into the ground, "distant fifteen yards one from the other," twelve of them in an equilateral triangle, and beneath one of them he buried a copper case containing his sword and the half disme coined from his own silver. Beneath one of them . . . But it was not beneath one of them. Or had it been? And had long ago been dug up by a Clarke? But the story had apparently died with Simeon and Sarah. On the other hand . . .

Ellery found himself irrationally reluctant to conclude the obvious. George Washington's lifelong absorption with figures kept intruding. Twelve trees, equidistant, in an equilateral triangle.

"What is it?" he kept asking himself, almost angrily. "Why isn't it satisfying me?"

And then, in the gathering dusk, a very odd explanation insinuated itself. *Because it wouldn't have satisfied him!*

That's silly, Ellery said to himself abruptly. It has all the earmarks of a satisfying experience. There is no more satisfying figure in all geometry than an equilateral triangle. It is closed, symmetrical, definite, a whole and balanced and finished thing.

But it wouldn't have satisfied George Washington . . . for all its symmetry and perfection.

Then perhaps there is a symmetry and perfection beyond the cold beauty of figures?

At this point, Ellery began to question his own postulates . . . lost in the dark and to his time . . .

They found him at ten-thirty, crouched on the cultivator seat, numb and staring.

He permitted himself to be led into the house, he suffered Nikki to subject him to the indignity of having his shoes and socks stripped off and his frozen feet rubbed to life, he ate Martha Clarke's dinner—all with a detachment and indifference which alarmed the girls and even made old Tobias look uneasy.

"If it's going to have this effect on him," began Martha, and then she said: "Ellery, give it up. Forget it." But she had to shake him before he heard her.

He shook his head. "They're there."

"Where?" cried the girls simultaneously.

"In Washington's Grove."

"Ye found 'em?" croaked Tobias Clarke, half-rising.

"No."

The Clarkes and Nikki exchanged glances.

"Then how can you be so certain they're buried there, Ellery?" asked Nikki gently.

Ellery looked bewildered. "Darned if I know *how* I know," he said, and he even laughed a little. "Maybe George Washington told me." Then he stopped laughing and went into the firelit parlor and—pointedly—slid the doors shut.

At ten minutes past midnight Martha Clarke gave up the contest.

"Isn't he *ever* going to come out of there?" she said, yawning.

"You never can tell what Ellery will do," replied Nikki.

"Well, I can't keep my eyes open another minute."

"Funny," said Nikki. "I'm not the least bit sleepy."

"You city girls."

"You country girls."

They laughed. Then they stopped laughing, and for a moment there was no sound in the kitchen but the patient sentry walk of the grandfather clock and the snores of Tobias assaulting the ceiling from above.

"Well," said Martha. Then she said: "I just *can't*. Are you staying up, Nikki?"

"For a little while. You go to bed, Martha."

"Yes. Well. Good night."

"Good night, Martha."

At the door Martha turned suddenly: "Did he say *George Washington* told him?"

"Yes."

Martha went rather quickly up the stairs.

Nikki waited fifteen minutes. Then she tiptoed to the foot of the stairs and listened. She heard Tobias snuffling and snorting as he turned over in his bed, and an uneasy moan from the direction of Martha's bedroom, as if she were dreaming an unwholesome dream. Nikki set her jaw grimly and went to the parlor doors and slid them open.

Ellery was on his knees before the fire. His elbows were resting on the floor. His face was propped in his hands. In this attitude his posterior was considerably higher than his head.

"Ellery!"

"Huh?"

"Ellery, what on earth—?"

"Nikki. I thought you'd gone to bed long ago." In the firelight his face was haggard.

"But what have you been *doing?* You look exhausted!"

"I am. I've been wrestling with a man who could bend a horseshoe with his naked hands. A very strong man. In more ways than one."

"What are you talking about? Who?"

"George Washington. Go to bed, Nikki."

"George . . . Washington?"

"Go to bed."

". . . *Wrestling* with him?"

"Trying to break through his defenses. Get into his mind. It's not an easy mind to get into. He's been dead such a long time— that makes the difference. The dead are stubborn, Nikki. Aren't you going to bed?"

Nikki backed out, shivering.

The house *was* icy.

It was even icier when an inhuman bellow accompanied by a thunder that shook the Revolutionary walls of her bedroom brought Nikki out of bed with a yelping leap.

But it was only Ellery.

He was somewhere up the hall, in the first glacial light of dawn, hammering on Martha's Clarke's door.

"Martha. *Martha!* Wake up, damn you, and tell me where I can find a book in this damned house! A biography of Washington—a history of the United States—an almanac . . . *anything!*"

The parlor fire had long since given up the ghost. Nikki and Martha in wrappers, and Tobias Clarke in an ancient bathrobe over his marbled long underwear, stood around shivering and bewildered as a disheveled, daemonic Ellery leafed eagerly through a 1921 edition of *The Farmer's Fact Book and Complete Compendium.*

"Here it is!" The words shot out of his mouth like bullets, leaving puffs of smoke.

"What is it, Ellery?"

"What on earth are you looking for?"

"He's loony, I tell ye!"

Ellery turned with a look of ineffable peace, closing the book. "That's it," he said. "That's it."

"What's it?"

"Vermont. The State of Vermont."

"Vermont . . . ?"

"Ver*mont?*"

"Vermont. What in the crawlin' creepers 's Vermont got to do with—?"

"Vermont," said Ellery with a tired smile, "did not enter the Union until March fourth, 1791. So that proves it, don't you see?"

"Proves *what?*" shrieked Nikki.

"Where George Washington buried his sword and half disme."

"Because," said Ellery in the rapidly lightening dawn behind the barn, "Vermont was the fourteenth State to do so. The *fourteenth*. Tobias would you get me an ax, please?"

"An ax," mumbled Tobias. He shuffled away, shaking his head.

"Come on, Ellery, I'm d-dying of c-cold!" chattered Nikki, dancing up and down before the cultivator.

"Ellery," said Martha Clarke piteously, "I don't understand *any* of this."

"It's very simple, Martha—oh, thank you, Tobias—as simple," said Ellery, "as simple arithmetic. Numbers, my dears—numbers tell this remarkable story. Numbers and their influence on our first President who was, above all things, a number-man. That was my key. I merely had to discover the lock to fit it into. Vermont was the lock. And the door's open."

Nikki seated herself on the cultivator. You had to give Ellery his head in a situation like this; you couldn't drive him for beans. Well, she thought grudgingly, seeing how pale and how tired-looking he was after a night's wrestling with George Washington, he's earned it.

"The number was wrong," said Ellery solemnly, leaning on Tobias's ax. "Twelve trees. Washington apparently planted twelve trees—Simeon Clarke's *Diary* never did mention the number twelve, but the evidence seemed unquestionable—there were twelve oaks in an equilateral triangle, each one fifteen yards from its neighbor.

"And yet . . . I felt that *twelve* oaks couldn't be, perfect as the triangle was. Not if they were planted by George Washington. Not on February the twenty-second, New Style, in the year of our Lord 1791.

"Because on February the twenty-second, 1791—in fact, until March the fourth, when Vermont entered the Union to swell its original number by one—there was *another* number in the United States so important, so revered, so much a part of the common speech and the common living—and dying—that it was more than a number; it was a solemn and sacred thing; almost not a number at all. It overshadowed other numbers like the still-unborn Paul Bunyan. It was memorialized on the new American flag in the number of its stars and the number of its stripes. It was a number of which George Washington was the standard-bearer!—the head and only recently the strong right arm of the new Republic which had been born out of the blood and muscle of its integers. It was a number which was in the hearts and minds and mouths of all Americans.

"No. If George Washington, who was not merely the living symbol of all this but carried with him that extraordinary compulsion toward numbers which characterized his whole temperament besides, had wished to plant a number of oak trees to commemorate a birthday visit in the year 1791 . . . he would have, he could have, selected only one number out of all the mathematical trillions at his command—*the number thirteen.*"

The sun was looking over the edge of Pennsylvania at Washington's Grove.

"George Washington planted thirteen trees here that day, and under one of them he buried Paul Revere's copper case. Twelve of the trees he arranged in an equilateral triangle, and we know that the historic treasure was not under any of the twelve. Therefore he must have buried the case under the thirteenth—a thirteenth oak sapling which grew to oakhood and, some time during the past century and a half, withered and died and vanished, vanished so utterly that it left no trace, not even its roots.

"Where would Washington have planted that thirteenth oak? Because beneath the spot where it once stood—there lies the copper case containing his sword and the first coin to be struck off in the new United States."

And Ellery glanced tenderly at the cherry sapling which Tobias

Clarke had set into the earth in the middle of Washington's Grove six years before.

"Washington the surveyor, the geometer, the man whose mind cried out for integral symmetries? Obviously, in only one place: *In the center of the triangle.* Any other place would be unthinkable."

And Ellery hefted Tobias's ax and strode toward the six-year-old tree. He raised the ax.

But suddenly he lowered it, and turned, and said in a rather startled way: "See here! isn't today . . . ?"

"Washington's Birthday," said Nikki.

Ellery grinned and began to chop down the cherry tree.

Q. Patrick appeared quite frequently in the periodicals of the forties and fifties, most notably in Ellery Queen's Mystery Magazine, *and his generally excellent tales should be collected on their own. Lieutenant Timothy Trant was a favorite Patrick protagonist in those years, appearing in many of his novels and short stories, several of which have appeared in this series. "Murder In One Scene" turns on an idea not unknown elsewhere in crime fiction— a man accidentally learns of the impending violent death of a stranger—but rarely has it had such adroit handling as here.*

Q. PATRICK

Murder in One Scene

Lieutenant Trant of the New York Homicide Bureau was dawdling over breakfast in his pleasant apartment. He buttered a piece of brioche and glanced at the three letters which had come in the mail.

They didn't look interesting. One was from his mother in Newport. He opened it and read Mrs. Trant's usual garrulous account of her social life with its usual undercurrent of pained surprise that her son should choose to be a New York policeman pursuing murderers when he might be escorting the toniest dowagers through the best drawing rooms of the Eastern seaboard.

The second letter came from a Princeton classmate who was starting a cultured magazine and thought Trant might like to sacrifice five hundred dollars on the altar of Art.

The third was even less promising. The long envelope bore his name and address in type and, on its left hand top corner, the printed words: *Big Pal.* Trant knew the organization. It was a worthy one which found sponsors for delinquent boys on parole. Lieutenant Trant, who preferred his criminals delinquent rather than rehabilitated, had no great desire to become a Big Pal. He slit the envelope, anticipating the printed plea beginning: *Dear Friend* . . .

But the envelope did not contain the usual form letter. Inside was a folded sheet of elegant blue stationery. Lieutenant Trant blinked. He unfolded the sheet and looked at what was written on it. He blinked again.

Beneath an embossed Park Avenue address had been written in a round feminine hand:

"Dear George:

"Since you insist, come at five tomorrow. But this is to warn you. I shall have Eddie there. I have also bought a gun. If you try what you tried last time, I will use it.

"Marna."

Lieutenant Trant, whose passion for the unorthodox was unbridled, smiled happily. Offhand he could think of nothing less orthodox than the arrival of so personal and interesting a communication in the envelope of an impersonal and unexciting charitable organization.

He realized that a mistake must have been made with envelopes. Appeals are usually sent out by volunteer ladies who have been given a sucker list and envelopes and who salve their social consciences by typing addresses and providing stamps. This particular volunteer lady—this unknown Marna—must have been very absent-minded or very jittery.

Judging by the nature of the letter she had mailed in the wrong envelope, she had been very jittery.

Trant looked at the date. It had been written the day before. "Five tomorrow" therefore meant five o'clock that afternoon. He let his thoughts toy pleasingly with a picture of the jittery Marna with her gun and Eddie waiting at five for the mysterious George who might "try" again what he had "tried" last time.

It was, of course, his duty as an officer of the law to investigate what might prove to be a very antisocial encounter.

He put the envelope and the letter in his pocket.

He was humming as he left his apartment . . .

A few minutes before five Lieutenant Trant, in an elegantly in-
conspicuous gray suit, arrived at the house whose address appeared at the head of Marna's letter. Although the house had a
Park Avenue number, its door was on a side street. It was an old
private residence which had been converted into apartments.

Since he did not know Marna's name, he stepped into the small
outside hall and studied the names above the door buzzers. There
was no Marna anything. Most of the names were discouraging.
But above the buzzer of the penthouse apartment were two printed
cards. One said: *Miss Joan Hyde.* The other said: *Mrs. George
Hyde.*

Marna could be Mrs. George Hyde. That would make her the
wife of the potentially sinister George. Miss Joan Hyde might be
her daughter. Lieutenant Trant was disappointed. Romantic about
mystery and the possibly mysterious, he had imagined Marna
blonde, beautiful—and young.

He was about to press the Hyde buzzer when a girl came in
from the street behind him and, fumbling through her pocketbook,
brought out a key and opened the door. She glanced at him ques-
tioningly and kept the door half open. He smiled and followed her
into the house.

The girl had started through the neat mirrored hallway toward a
self-service elevator, but she stopped and turned back to him a little suspiciously.

"Are you looking for someone?"

She was young and pretty with shining dark hair, cool eyes and
a sort of lazy self-assurance which went with the silver fox coat
she was wearing.

How nice, thought Lieutenant Trant, if Marna had looked like
that.

He said: "As a matter of fact, I'm looking for Marna Hyde."

"Oh." She smiled. "How interesting."

"Is it?"

"To me it is." She moved to the elevator. "I'll take you up."

Lieutenant Trant got into the elevator, too. The girl's perfume
was pleasant. As she made the elevator ascend, she glanced at him
sidewise.

"Don't say Marna's got herself a new beau."

"Do I look like a beau?"

"Very. But I wouldn't have thought Marna'd have the energy to take on a new man—what with George to get rid of and the faithful Eddie hovering."

So far so good, thought Lieutenant Trant.

The elevator reached the top floor. They got out to face a single door. The girl started to fumble in her pocketbook again.

"So you live here, too," said Trant.

"I moved in when George moved out. I'm a bodyguard. Hasn't Marna mentioned me? I'm Joan."

"George's sister."

"Yes."

"And you're not on George's side?"

"About the divorce?" Joan Hyde turned. "Are you kidding?"

"I never kid," said Lieutenant Trant. "I am a very sedate young man."

Joan Hyde had found the key. "I don't imagine Marna's home yet but come in and have a drink."

"I'd like to very much."

She opened the door, chattering: "I've just been to that French movie with Barrault and Arletty. It's quite wonderful, but at the beginning I never dreamed he wouldn't get her at the end. Why are foreign movies always so gloomy?"

Trant followed her into a charmingly casual living room. His trained eye saw several very valuable pieces.

Joan Hyde said: "It's nothing much. They wanted a hangout in New York and Marna brought up some of the junk from their Long Island attic. I'll rustle up a drink. Sit down."

As the girl disappeared into the kitchen, Trant moved to a small Chippendale breakfront desk, reflecting that anyone who had "junk" like this in a Long Island attic had no financial problems. On the desk he saw what he hoped he would see. Beside a portable typewriter, there was a pile of unused *Big Pal* envelopes; a pile of form letters; a mimeographed list of addresses; and a second neat pile of letters which had been addressed on the typewriter and stamped ready for mailing.

He glanced at the name on the top and saw that a Mr. and Mrs. LeRoy Jones of Seventy-eighth Street were about to be urged to take an interest in delinquent boys. He had just enough time to glance at the letter below which was for a Mrs. Samuel Katzenbach when he heard Joan returning and dropped into a chair.

"I'm afraid there's only rye." Joan Hyde appeared with a tray. "After having put up with George for so long, Marna and I are a little cautious about alcohol." She put the tray down and glanced at him curiously. "I suppose you do know what I'm talking about? You're not someone who's come to look at the plumbing, are you?"

"I was never good with my hands," said Lieutenant Trant.

Joan made drinks and chattered on. As Trant listened, the situation became increasingly clear. Marna had married George. George was a drunk. Marna had met Eddie. Marna had wanted a divorce. The drunken George had made terrible scenes; at one time he had drunkenly tried to kill Marna. Joan, entirely sympathetic with her sister-in-law, had moved in as protection.

"It's dreary," meditated Joan. "You can't help feeling fond of your own brother, but George is quite frightening. And he still has a key. I'm always telling Marna she should get the lock changed. But she's always putting it off. I . . . ."

Trant was losing interest. In spite of the fascinating accident which had made him conscious of it, this was basically a trite situation. A wealthy alcoholic with a temper; probably a frivolous wife.

His thought train snapped because a noise had come from the room, presumably a bedroom, behind Joan. It was a very slight sound but enough to tell him someone was there.

He glanced at his watch. "Five-ten. Marna made a fuss about my being on time. You don't suppose she's in the bedroom? Maybe asleep?"

Joan put her drink down. "I strenuously doubt it. Want me to look?"

"Would you?"

A newspaper lay on the arm of Trant's chair. To feign indifference he picked it up and glanced at it. It had been turned to a review of the opening of the circus. He looked down the columns.

Joan Hyde reached the bedroom door. She opened it. She gasped. "Marna!"

Instantly Trant ran to her side. Oblivious of him, Joan took a step into the room. Trant followed. A blonde girl in a black dress sat huddled on one of the twin beds. Her hair tumbled in disorder around her beautiful but stricken face. Fantastically she was wearing white suede gloves and over the knuckles of the right hand glove stretched a red damp stain.

Joan ran to her. "Marna, what's the matter?"

Trant gazed as if hypnotized at the red stain. Marna turned to look at him from blank eyes.

"Joan, tell that man to go."

"But, Marna, he has a date with you."

"Tell him to go away."

Trant took a step forward, his eyes darting about the room. He passed the foot of the bed. He moved toward the window.

Marna jumped up and screamed: "No, no."

He came to the second bed. He looked down at the area of carpet between the bed and the window. Sprawled on his stomach was the body of a young man. A revolver lay on the floor close to him.

The back of his head had been shot away. He was dead. There was no doubt about that.

Joan came running to Trant's side. "George!" she cried. "Oh, Marna, he tried to attack you again. He . . ."

Trant turned to Marna Hyde. She stood quite still. She was as lovely as he could have wanted her to be.

Rather sadly he said: "Since you bought the gun, Mrs. Hyde, I suppose you felt you should get your money's worth."

Both the girls were staring at him.

He added: "By the way, do you always wear gloves in the house?"

"She has a milk allergy." It was Joan who spoke. "Her hands broke out again this afternoon. She always wears gloves when it's bad. But—who are you? Why are you here?"

Trant shrugged. "I'm sorry to give you such good service. I'm from the Homicide Bureau." He took Marna's elbow. "Shall we move into the next room?"

Marna let him guide her into the living room. She dropped into a chair. Joan Hyde came after them.

"Homicide Bureau. I don't understand."

"You're not meant to." Trant was watching Marna. "You have been sending out appeals for the *Big Pal* people, haven't you?"

The girl shivered. She did not seem to have heard the question. He repeated it. She whispered: "Yes."

"You sent some off yesterday and did some more today?"

"Yes."

Trant took from his pocket the letter he had received and handed it to her.

"You wrote this, Mrs. Hyde?"

"Yes, but how . . . ?"

"It's all fairly obvious, isn't it? Your husband didn't want the divorce. He'd been acting violently. He was coming at five. You were afraid of him so you bought a gun. He got violent again. You shot him."

Marna Hyde did not say anything.

Trant went on: "There's just one thing that seems to be missing. Eddie was supposed to be here. Where is he?"

Marna was looking at the blood stain on her glove. There was dead silence. The buzzer shrilled. Joan started for the door, but Trant outdistanced her to the hall. He opened the door onto a blond young man with broad shoulders and very blue eyes.

Trant said: "Hello, Eddie."

The young man glared. "Who are you?"

"Just a stray policeman. You're a little late for the murder."

"Murder? Nothing's—nothing's happened to Marna?"

Roughly the young man pushed past Trant and ran into the living room. Trant followed. The young man hurried to Marna and dropped at her side, his face gaunt with anxiety.

"Marna, baby. Marna, are you all right?"

"It's George, Eddie," said Joan. "He's dead."

Marna turned so that she was looking straight at the young man. "Eddie, you didn't . . . ?" Slowly the expression of horror faded from her eyes. "No." She got up and confronted Trant. She seemed almost calm.

"I haven't any idea how you got here, but presumably you want to ask me questions. It's all quite simple. I did buy the gun. I did write George that letter. But that's all I did. I've been out this afternoon. I got back just before five. I went into the bedroom. I—I found George. I was still bending over him when I heard Joan come in with you. I heard a strange voice. It was all a terrible shock. I didn't want a stranger involved. I decided to wait in the bedroom until you had gone."

Lieutenant Trant lit a cigarette. He was thinking hard and he discovered that he was beginning to relish this situation which, whatever it turned out to be, was no longer trite.

He sat down on the arm of a chair. All three of them were watching him as if he were a time bomb.

He glanced at Marna. "So that's your story. Your husband was dead when you came home?"

"It's true."

Trant smiled. "You would hardly admit that it was a lie, Mrs. Hyde. Of course, with those gloves, there'd be no fingerprints on the gun. You picked a lucky time for your disagreement with milk."

"Marna's milk allergy is on the level," barked Eddie. "Show him your hands, Marna."

Marna peeled off her right glove. There was no doubt about the allergy. Her thumb, the tips of her second and first fingers and the whole middle of her palm were sprinkled with little white blisters. She turned the hand over. Her knuckles were split. She put the glove on again.

Lieutenant Trant looked apologetic. "I'm sorry, Mrs. Hyde. I shouldn't have doubted your word." He eyed her almost with affection. "I might as well explain my presence. There's no magic involved. I'm on the *Big Pal* sucker list. This morning I got what should have been the appeal. It wasn't. I got George's letter instead. I came to see what would happen here at five o'clock."

The drinks were still on the tray. Eddie poured himself a shot of straight rye. Neither of the girls spoke.

"I thought," continued Trant, "that I had received the letter by mistake. That, of course, was what I was supposed to think. Unhappily, I don't think it any more."

Marna said: "What do you think?"

Trant did not reply. "When you're sending out appeals to people on an alphabetical list, the only way to do it without driving yourself crazy is to send them in alphabetical order."

"That's what I did."

"Exactly. Yesterday you got up to the I's. I took a look at your desk. Today you began with the J's and K's. My name's Trant. Certainly you hadn't got to the T's yesterday. You couldn't inadvertently have put George's letter in an envelope for me by yesterday."

Eddie asked: "Which means?"

"That the letter was sent to me by-mistake-on-purpose. Some-one saw my name on the sucker list and knew my reputation as a sort of crackpot policeman. They knew if I received the letter I'd be intrigued enough to show up here at five."

The two girls together asked: "But why?"

"Because they wanted me to come. The letter would have given me a preconceived idea of motive. I would have found George's body and realized right away that he had attacked his wife and she had shot him in self-defense. I would have written George off as a victim of justifiable homicide. I might even have made a little speech to Mrs. Hyde about Valiant American Womanhood. Yes, it was a neat trap, a very neat trap."

Eddie asked belligerently: "Are you suggesting that Marna . . ."

"I'm not suggesting that Mrs. Hyde did anything at all." Trant looked at Eddie. "Do you have a key to this apartment?"

"Of course I don't."

"But you were hoping to marry Mrs. Hyde once she got the di-vorce?"

He flushed. "I was and I am."

Trant turned to Marna. "I imagine your husband was quite rich."

"He was very well off."

"Seems to have been a kind of irresponsible character. Didn't make the money himself, did he?"

"No. It's a trust. When his parents died, they left it all to him in trust. He can't touch the capital. Just the income."

Lieutenant Trant was still watching Marna. "Lucky accident my arrival coincided with your sister-in-law's, wasn't it? If I'd come a minute earlier, you wouldn't have let me in. If I'd arrived a min-ute later, you'd have told Joan about George and you would not have let anyone in either."

Trant continued musingly: "I always rather suspect lucky acci-dents. They're not always as accidental as they seem."

He shifted his quiet attention to Joan Hyde. "You live here, Miss Hyde. Perhaps you saw Marna writing that letter to George yesterday. Perhaps you even offered to mail it."

Joan Hyde looked back at him blankly.

"I suppose," he went on in his soft, almost gentle voice, "you called George in Marna's name and asked him to come a little before five. After you'd killed him, you went downstairs, saw Marna come home and waited for me. That was an ingenious device, assuming I was a beau of Marna's. It gave you a chance to sell me once and for all on the manslaughter set-up. The violent George, the unchanged lock . . ."

Her dark eyes blazing, Joan snapped: "You're mad."

Lieutenant Trant looked disappointed. "Why do murderers always say: *You're mad?* Do you suppose they pick it up in the movies?"

"You . . ."

"In any case, I'm afraid the movies have been your downfall, Miss Hyde. You got just a little too chatty about your French film. You told me you never dreamed at the beginning that Barrault wouldn't get Arletty in the end. To be in doubt about the end of a movie at the beginning proves quite definitely that you saw the beginning first."

He picked up the newspaper from the arm of the chair. "That French movie happens to be playing at only one Manhattan house. I notice here in the timetable that it begins at 1:20, 3:20 and 5:20. Since you saw the beginning before the end you could not possibly have seen the 3:20 show and arrived here just before five. If you went to the movie at all today, you went to the show which was over just before 3:20. That gave you plenty of time to eliminate George." He paused. "That does horrid things to your alibi, doesn't it?"

Joan Hyde seemed stunned. So did Eddie and Marna.

Eddie asked: "But why would Joan . . . ?"

"Failing offspring, a trust fund reverts to the family." Trant's amiable gaze moved to Marna. "Am I right in assuming that Miss Hyde is the family?"

"Why, yes," faltered Marna. "She's the only other child. I suppose the trust goes to her."

"Money." Lieutenant Trant sighed. "Such an orthodox motive. Perhaps you'd give me the name of your husband's lawyer. Just to check."

He produced a pencil and a piece of paper. Marna took the pencil in her right hand and scribbled. Trant put the paper in his pocket. He was still watching Marna.

"When you discovered the corpse, you thought Eddie must have done it, didn't you? Once you'd realized no court would convict you, you'd almost certainly have taken the rap for his sake. Yes, it was quite an expert little scheme for disposing of an alcoholic brother and living happily ever after on his trust fund."

He moved to Joan Hyde. He always felt a slight pang when the time came to arrest an attractive and clever murderess.

She was still quite calm and her eyes were hard with anger. "You'll never prove it. Never."

Trant grinned. "You'll be surprised at what I can prove when I put my mind to it. For example, we've hardly scratched that milk allergy, have we?"

He turned to Marna. "Would you take off your glove again?"

The girl obeyed. Trant drew Joan toward her sister-in-law.

"Your sister-in-law wrote down the lawyer's name for me. See how the pressure of the pencil broke those little blisters? Blisters are very sensitive, Miss Hyde. I challenge even you to have fired a gun and kept your blisters intact." He shrugged. "Mrs. Hyde couldn't have fired the gun. Eddie, who didn't have a key, couldn't have got in. So . . . Like me to do some more proving?"

Eddie was gazing at Marna's hand. He muttered: "For heaven's sake, he's proved it, Marna. It took him just ten minutes."

Trant had a firm hold on Joan Hyde's arm. He still liked her perfume.

"A good detective," he said modestly, "would have solved it before it happened. It's too bad, Miss Hyde. If I'd been a little brighter, we might be going to the theater tonight, instead of to the Tombs . . ."

In a notable stroke of genius R. Austin Freeman, in The Singing
Bone *(1912), created what has come to be known as the inverted
detective story. The inverted form is particularly exacting in its
demands on the writer: he must disclose the identity of the murderer at the outset and yet maintain suspense and reader interest
through the ensuing detection of the crime. Though "The Million-to-One Chance," from the 1950 anthology, is not inverted
detection in this sense, hanging as it does upon the recognition of
the significance of a single incident—it well approaches the form
and, as with the classic inverted story, offers the challenge to the
reader: by what flaw(s) in his scheme is the culprit tripped up?*

ROY VICKERS

The Million-to-One Chance

"Acting on information received,"—the *cliché* which means that a
copper's nark, or other informer, has pulled Scotland Yard out of
a difficulty—the police located the corpse of Arthur Crouch some
six months after the murder. It was, from the police point of view,
a nice, tidy murder, with no loose ends. Locate the corpse and you
had located the murderer.

Oddly enough, it was not the murder but the *cliché* which
caused the scandal, the questions in Parliament, the public hulla-
baloo. *How* had the information been received? The circumstances
of the crime excluded the possibility of a witness at any stage.
Something, it seemed, was being covered up.

Nobody suggested that Stretton might be innocent of the murder: his guilt was obvious. Nobody wanted to know the name and

address of the informer. But nearly everybody wanted to be assured that, in this case, the *cliché* was true—that a person or persons existed who had told Scotland Yard where the body was to be found.

It was the Animal Lovers League that set the snowball rolling —due to the fact that Crouch happened to have a dog with him when he was murdered. And the dog happened to be a mastiff! The legendary dog of England, now as rare a spectacle as a horse-drawn carriage! A huge, fierce animal, looking even fiercer than it is—in appearance suggesting a bulldog the size of a Great Dane.

The breed of the dog swelled the publicity. The public was reminded that mastiffs used to board the Spanish galleons with Drake's men—that Nelson was afraid of them, and banished them from the Navy.

And here, in 1937, was a mastiff turning up in a murder mystery—but in the strange role of informer. Indeed, the Animal Fans believed that this dog was able to reason that its master had been murdered: that it understood it must therefore communicate with the police: that it had persisted in its efforts for more than six months—only to be shot by Scotland Yard when it had nobly done its duty.

This sob-story of the Martyred Mastiff—with a near-human mentality—was even accepted by many who were not dog-minded, because it was the simplest way of dodging a dilemma.

Crouch, who lived in Hampstead, North London, came out of his house, leading the mastiff, in the late afternoon of July 23rd, his car being parked nearby. A schoolboy of fifteen, who stopped to gape at the mastiff, testified that Crouch shouted to a man who had just strolled past the house, apparently a friend. The boy's interest was on the dog, so he had observed only that the other man was "big" and that Crouch was "little."

On one essential point the boy was positive. Crouch, the victim, had persuaded the big man—presumed to be the murderer—to enter the car. "Be generous, and let's use my car," Crouch said. The words had stuck in the boy's memory because he had thought it a funny way to talk about giving a man a lift.

At dawn the car had been found in Central London. But the man and the dog—which was taller, on its hind legs, than the man, and substantially heavier—had disappeared, leaving no traces whatever. Nothing relevant was discovered in six months. Then—*presto!*—the whole case was cleaned up in a few hours.

The tall man who had been persuaded to enter the car was Dennis Stretton. He was an engineer, of some minor distinction, in his early forties. He and Crouch had been fellow students and close friends. Stretton had graduated with a First; Crouch, who had taken only a Fourth, subsequently specialized in the finance of engineering. Their friendship had never been formally broken, but they had not seen each other for seven years.

A news paragraph had misinformed Stretton that Crouch was away on holiday with his wife—his second wife—or Stretton would not have been loitering outside Crouch's house in Hampstead.

He had come solely to indulge his own morbid melancholy. He wanted to gloat over the house in which Crouch lived—more precisely, the house in which Crouch had lived with the late Mrs. Crouch, who had died some eighteen months previously. The late Mrs. Crouch—a wistful, attractive Belgian—had been engaged to Stretton before she married Crouch seven years ago.

The car was parked some dozen yards up the road, so Stretton missed its significance. Crouch, coming out suddenly with the mastiff, had spotted him before he had gone three full paces.

"Dennis!" he called.

It would have been ridiculous to walk on as if he had not heard. Stretton turned round, startled into speechlessness as much by the bull-head of the mastiff, flush with Crouch's hip, as by the awkwardness of the meeting.

"I say, Dennis, we don't have to cut each other, do we?" Crouch added: "I've missed you like the devil!"

"It's very civil of you to say that, Arthur." He did not believe that Crouch had missed him. "The 'Journal' said you were in Sussex, or I—"

"Driving down this evening. I'm on my way to park poor old Oscar with the vet for ten days." Pointless conversation, which showed that Crouch, too, felt the strain, though he could, Stretton reminded himself, talk his way out of anything. "Look here, Dennis, let's be frank with each other, as we used to be. I know there's a certain atmosphere which nothing I can say will dispel. All the same, I'm going to ask you a favor."

"By all means!" When you felt as Stretton felt, no satisfaction could be obtained from mere discourtesy.

"I'm having a ghastly job with the Belgian Probate people to wind up poor Leonie's estate. Red tape about identification—and I wonder if you would be good enough to help?"

"Me! How could I possibly help?"

"Leonie told me once that you never returned her passport."

"Didn't I?" Stretton was trying to remember.

Crouch went on: "As we were married in Belgium, we used mine—endorsed with her married name, of course. Her original passport is about the only means of convincing them that Leonie Crouch was once Leonie de Ripert."

"If I still have it, I know where it must be. I'll send it to you."

This was not what Crouch wanted.

"Could I come with you and collect it now, Dennis? The thing is becoming a nightmare. Marion—my present wife—keeps worrying me to get it all settled."

"But I've given up my flat. I'm living in a remote cottage in Essex—by the marshes. Open air life. Doctor's orders. It's fifteen miles the other side of London. With the traffic, it'll take you more than an hour and a half to get there."

"It doesn't matter what time I turn up at my father-in-law's place. I can have dinner on my way down." He added: "Be generous, and let's use my car."

Crouch could put an infernal persuasiveness into his voice. Again and again in the past Stretton had let himself against his will be talked into agreement.

"Very well! But we may find that I haven't got the passport." He looked at the mastiff with misgiving. "D'you want to park the dog with the vet first?"

"No. Two sides of a triangle. Quicker to drop him after I leave you."

He opened the rear door of the car. The mastiff ambled in and bestowed himself on the floor.

"Make for the other side of dockland—near Tillbury—and then I'll pilot you," said Stretton as he got in beside Crouch. "I'm right in the wilds on the north bank of the river."

Crouch skirted North London, driving eastwards. Now and again they exchanged commonplace remarks—thrown, as it were, over the wall of hatred between them.

In a long traffic block, Crouch leaned over and patted the mastiff. The dog yawned. Crouch glanced from the huge jaws to Stretton's throat. For it was Crouch, the victim, who had the psychology of a murderer—the kind of murderer who kills slowly; and without tangible weapons.

As students they had been normal young men of more than average promise, normal in their friendship, with a touch of honest, unconcealed jealousy on Crouch's part.

In the 1914 war they were in the same Technical Company. On their way out the troopship had been torpedoed, when Crouch's nerve had failed rather lamentably, and Stretton, at some risk of his own life, had saved him from drowning.

It may be doubted whether any man can feel unalloyed gratitude to another for saving his life. He is apt to regard his rescuer as a moral creditor who can never be paid off. In the special circumstances—notably the circumstance of Crouch's panic—Stretton had incidentally committed the offense of revealing a definite superiority.

Thereafter their relationship had changed, but so subtly that Stretton had been unaware of it. Crouch persuaded himself that he detected patronage in the other's manner. He hid his resentment, used it as fuel to the inner fire which burned steadily for the rest of his life.

For ten years following return to civil life, Stretton did not know that Crouch had become his enemy: once or twice he had his suspicions, but Crouch talked his way out. It was not until Crouch actually married Leonie that the truth flashed upon Stretton. Even then he did not understand why. Stretton had, almost literally, forgotten the life-saving episode.

The first outstanding incident occurred when Stretton was given a favorable opportunity to acquire a junior partnership. While he was completing arrangements with his bank manager, he was informed that the opportunity had been snapped up by another—who turned out to be Crouch. But Crouch had explained that away.

Later, Stretton leased patent rights in an invention of his own —a valuable adaptation of the steam turbine—to Harmoddle, Limited, who intended to put the engine into immediate production. A few weeks later Crouch became Chairman of Harmoddle's. The patent rights were retained: the penalties for nonproduction were paid quarterly. But Stretton's engine was kept off the market. Crouch explained that away, too.

In the course of professional visits to Brussels, Stretton met and eventually proposed marriage to Leonie. Owing to the strict religious views of her family they had decided to marry without religious ceremony in England. During some slight routine delay which he encountered in connection with her passport she wrote breaking off the engagement and begging him not to see her again.

Stretton did not grieve very much at the time. Her harsh and arbitrary rejection of him even inclined him to the view that he had had a lucky escape, notwithstanding her very considerable physical attractiveness.

Six months later Crouch, having converted himself to the religious views of her family, married her ceremonially in Belgium.

Instantly, the frustrations of the last ten years were floodlit. Stretton derided himself as a credulous fool who had let Crouch on his shoulders to steal or to spoil the prizes.

There was no showdown, no harsh words, nothing in the nature of a quarrel. It was as if their friendship had merely lapsed. Stretton settled down to the kind of passive, well-mannered hatred that rarely harms its object but acts as slow poison in the brain of the hater.

He stood well in his profession, but his career had its ups and downs: when the slow poison got to work he debited all the downs to Crouch. Leonie became the symbol of his blighted life. The memory of her physical beauty began to torture his imagination, shutting out the possibility of his seeking other women. In the background of this obsession was some kind of belief that she would one day come to him. When he learned of her death he had a nervous breakdown.

After some weeks in a nursing home he was advised to knock off work for a year and live a simple and muscular life in the open air. He bought the cottage in Essex, standing by itself on the fringe of the marsh, where he dug and re-dug the garden, occasionally shooting duck and occasionally sailing in the Thames estuary.

Within a year of Leonie's death he learned from the personal column of an engineering journal that Crouch had married again. The same column misinformed him that Crouch had joined his wife for a short vacation at her father's house in Sussex.

His physical health had been greatly improved, but the vision of Leonie persisted, finally driving him to look at the outside of the house in which another had enjoyed her charms.

Sunk in his own thoughts, Stretton forgot to function as pilot when they reached and passed Tillbury. Within half a mile of the cottage it dawned on him that Crouch had taken the correct route off the main road, through the lanes.

He had not given Crouch the name of the cottage. Even with that information a stranger would have to inquire, or to put in some close work with an ordnance map.

They were now in a very lonely spot. Linked with the realization of Crouch's odd behavior was acute consciousness of the mastiff lying on the floor behind, separated only by the back of the bucket seat. Stretton felt a prickling in his spine. He would have concealed his feeling, but for a mischance of the road.

The whole incident was over in a few seconds. A shaggy, white-coated sheepdog burst through the hedge almost under the wheels of the car. Crouch braked hard. The mastiff sprang up with a whine. A sound like a muffled scream broke from Stretton.

"Sorry!" exclaimed Crouch. "Couldn't help it." From the other's tone Stretton felt sure he had betrayed himself.

Ahead, the lane dipped into a stream some ten feet wide.

"Can I get through, Dennis?"

He knew he could get through, thought Stretton, because he had been here before. But he answered:

"You'll be all right if you take it very slowly. It's only a cattle-ford."

To himself his voice had sounded wobbly. The mastiff was sitting on its haunches, looking through the windscreen, its head between those of the two men. Stretton was nauseated by the creature's breath. He was still unsure of his voice, felt he must put it to the test.

"Don't let your megatherium jump out of the window and eat that sheepdog," he said, as Crouch slowed to walking pace for the ford, "or the farmers will smoke me out."

"Oscar would never fight until I told him to," laughed Crouch. "And then he'd fight anything."

The laugh rasped Stretton's nerve. No unarmed man would stand a chance against that animal. And Crouch was putting on an act, of some sort.

"They're a fighting breed, you know," prattled Crouch. "That is, they hold their bite until they can land on a vital spot. They've rather outlived their day—there are less than a dozen in the whole country."

They cleared the ford and at the next bend came to the cottage.

"You'll have to drive right in, or you'll block the lane. Not that anybody ever comes out this way."

He found himself wishing he had not made the last remark. Then common sense steadied him. If Crouch were to set the mastiff on him, it would be murder. Crouch might get away, but the police would know that a mastiff had been used; and as there were less than a dozen in the country they would soon pick him out, and Crouch would be hanged.

"You can park at the side of the cottage—then it will be easy to back and turn."

As Crouch stepped out of the car, the mastiff put its head through the open window. With something between a slither and a leap it landed in the garden, stretched, sniffed the air.

"Oscar had better stay in the car," said Crouch, and opened the rear door. "Oscar—guard!"

Instead of obeying the mastiff cringed and whined.

"Why, what's the matter, old boy?" He patted the dog and talked nonsense to it. But when he again ordered it into the car it circled round him, fawning and whimpering in canine apology for disobeying an order.

"Something's upsetting him." Crouch was puzzled. "Dennis, d'you mind if I touch you? I want to show him we're friends." Crouch put his hands on Stretton's shoulders. "There, there! Dear Dennis! Nice Dennis!" In his preposterous pantomine of affection Crouch stood on tiptoe and went through the motions of administering a kiss.

The mastiff ignored the whole performance. Only when Crouch bellowed at him did he slink back into the car.

Crouch slammed the door—but he did not, Stretton noticed, shut the window. The dog could come if Crouch were to call him.

"Those scientific tests of the dog's intelligence are damned unscientific!" he exclaimed. "They're tests for elementary human intelligence. Dogs haven't got any. Take Oscar. He only understands seven words, and he thinks all policemen are sugar-daddies, because a constable petted him when he was a puppy. All the same, they understand the devil of a lot in their own way. I believe they have a thought-pattern which we can't analyze."

"Afraid I've never had any feeling for animals," returned Stretton, his fear subsiding. "Shall we go in?"

It was a spacious little five-roomed cottage, incongruously furnished with items from Stretton's London flat. The front window of the parlor looked over marshland to the Thames. From the side window, when Crouch's car was not blocking the view, could be seen only a meagre wood, which screened the nearest neighbor half a mile away.

"Only fifteen miles from London and not a human habitation in sight!" Crouch, lounging in a very urban armchair, was making conversation. "You're pretty snug here, Dennis. D'you do your own housework?"

Stretton had taken a deed box from what was once a cocktail cabinet. He had already produced whiskey. Quarrel with Crouch or treat him as an ordinary guest—there could be no middle course.

"A woman comes on a push-bike three days a week to clean up and cook me a joint."

Stretton unlocked the deed box, untied the string of a small parcel marked with an initial. L for Leonie.

Crouch raised his glass.

"Whatever may be wrong with your health, old man, may it soon pass!"

"Thanks!" With his back to Crouch he opened the small parcel, and saw that Leonie had been right about the passport. It would be petty to pretend he had not found it.

"That's what you want, Arthur."

"I'm enormously obliged, Dennis!" If Crouch had put the passport in his pocket he would probably have departed unharmed. But he flourished it and talked about it.

"Thundering good likeness for a passport photo!" Crouch turned the pages. "Ah, this is what we want: *'Leonie Therese de Ripert: Parents: Alphonse Marie de Ripert—'* "

It was the fluttering of the pages that stirred the chord of memory. Stretton had supplied all those details, in triplicate, to British and to Belgian authorities. Obviously, a Belgian lawyer could settle the whole thing from the files.

"Arthur, why did you really want to come here?" Stretton's

voice was steady: so was his hand when he took up his whiskey. "The passport story is punk."

"My dear fellow!"

"You've been around here before, in my absence."

"How can you possibly suggest that?"

"You forgot to ask me the route."

It would take him some time to talk that away, thought Stretton, but again he was wrong.

"You win, Dennis. I plead guilty to a pious fraud." He drained his glass. "I told you I had missed you like the devil. I couldn't approach you while Leonie was alive. After her death I heard you were ill—and I guessed what had pulled you down. I had to find out how things were with you."

The same old technique—an explanation that could be neither proved nor disproved. In reality Crouch had probably come to gloat over his handiwork.

"And now that you have found out?"

"I want to know whether I can be of any help to you, Dennis —in any way whatever?"

"Thanks, Arthur, you can!" At the expression in the other's eyes Stretton's last doubt vanished. He laughed offensively. "It's not going to be a request for a loan. It's going to be a request for truth. It will help me to straighten things out in my own mind if you will tell me the truth about Leonie."

Crouch shrugged as if with embarrassment. To lengthen the silence he poured himself another drink. So Leonie had hurt— perhaps could be made to hurt a little more! Even by telling the truth.

"The truth, I'm afraid, was well known to most of our acquaintances. There are no lurid details. We just bored each other beyond bearing. Unfortunately for us both, her religious principles put divorce out of reach."

Stretton was aware of a thudding in his ears. The suppression of his invention—all the disappointments, real and imaginary, in which he had seen the hand of Crouch—were concentrated in the now tragic figure of Leonie.

"So you spoiled her life without even getting any pleasure yourself in doing so!"

"That's very bitter, old man! And it's exaggerated. It wasn't all gloom. There was the honeymoon era—"

"Stop!" The word cracked like a whiplash. Crouch was beginning to be alarmed by the extent of his own success.

"I think I'd better go now, Dennis. We ought not have talked about her. But you demanded the truth."

"I'm still demanding it, Arthur. What filthy lie about me did you tell her to make her throw me down as if I had been a moral leper?"

Crouch set down his glass unfinished and got up.

"I told no lies about you. I did not approach her until after she had jilted you."

Stretton cut off his line to the door.

"What filthy lie did you tell her about me?" It was as if he had been repeating that question for seven years. "Answer that and you can get out of here and we need never see each other again."

"I have already explained—"

"You dirty little rat, you'll tell me if I have to choke it out of you!" He gripped Crouch by the throat, thrust him back into the armchair, and with his knees on the other's thighs, bent his head back over the arm of the chair. "It must have been a filthy lie, or she would have asked for a showdown. You wanted her solely in order to take her away from me. Answer—d'you hear!—or I'll choke you. Speak, you little fool! *Speak!"*

He had not choked Crouch but broken his neck.

Part of him was bewildered, still waiting for Crouch's confession, wondering why he did not say something. But another part of him knew that he had intended to kill Crouch for saying that Leonie was a bore—except on the honeymoon.

He stood back, getting his breath, staring at the wreckage in the armchair.

"My God! I've forgotten his damned dog!"

No unarmed man would stand a chance against that animal. There came a different kind of thudding in his ears now, which might have been made by the pads of the mastiff in the hallway of the cottage. Had the front door been left open? He couldn't remember.

"It will see Arthur through the window, then jump through the glass."

He caught up a rug and flung it over what had been Crouch.

He looked through the front window—from one side, then from

the other to widen his angle—and saw nothing. He crossed to the side window, stepping over the feet of the corpse.

"Maybe I can see into the car."

The brute was not sitting, or it would have been visible. By standing on a couple of thick books he was able to see part of the floor of the car.

"It's not there. Then it must be prowling round the cottage looking for its master. Or in the hall, waiting for him to come out of this room."

The thudding in his ears produced the illusion of any sound that panic conjured up. Wherever he feared the dog might be, there he heard it. In the garden—scratching on the wall—padding about upstairs.

The gun, with which he occasionally shot wild duck, was upstairs in the bedroom.

He knelt and peered through the keyhole. Was the beast crouching to spring as soon as the door was opened?

"It can't know what has happened, or it would bark, or something." Also, he remembered, Crouch had had no chance to call it. "Have to risk it!"

He opened the door, found nothing in the hallway. But the front door was open. If he could get upstairs he would be safe. He shut the parlor door behind him, then rushed the stairs.

He slammed the bedroom door and stood, panting, for some seconds. There was a box of cartridges under the bed. When he had loaded, panic passed, leaving him free to face the fact that he had not killed Crouch in self-defense. Nor would anyone believe that it had been accidental.

He was cool now, even self-possessed. Crouch had been on his way to Sussex: had changed his plans after he came out of his house. Therefore no one knew where Crouch had gone.

"Better locate that dog and let him have both barrels."

Holding the gun like an infantryman mopping-up, he skirted the cottage, then the garden, then looked again in the car to make sure.

"Where are you? Come out, you brute, and fight."

With the gun in his hand he no longer feared the teeth of the mastiff. Yet in some way the animal was dominating him, mocking both his scientific training and his common sense. He was aware that his hands were sweating, while his spine was cold and prickling.

He was fighting the eerie feeling that the dog had gone to summon the police.

He forced a laugh, but the idea refused to seem as absurd as it ought to seem. Crouch had said something about a thought-pattern, different from human intelligence.

And something about this particular dog being specially fond of policemen.

In a quarter of an hour the scientific training and the common sense had prevailed, and he was able to make rational arrangements.

The marsh, he knew, would be useless as a hiding place for the body. A few hours of rain and the whole waste became a network of rivulets, all swirling into the highway of the Thames. It would have to be the garden, the potato bed. The earth there was deep and soft.

It was nearly seven when he started digging, the loaded shotgun within arm's reach. The moon would rise at ten fifty-seven. He must fill the grave before then. Not that he feared observation. But he would prefer to bury Crouch with as little light as possible, for the sake of his own unsteady nerve.

In this he was successful. When he had finished digging there was just enough light for his purpose.

He returned to the cottage, gritted his teeth, and set about his task. In his preoccupation with the corpse he had forgotten the risk of the mastiff appearing and taking him by surprise.

The grave was some fifteen feet from the large shed that served him as a garage. On the return journey, with his burden, he had to pass near the tail of Crouch's car, parked between the cottage and the garage. That reminded him that he had left the shotgun at the grave side.

For a moment he stood still, paralyzed by physical fear of the mastiff. Then, hampered as he was, he ran. An hysterical sob broke from him as he found the shotgun. He turned at bay, his finger round the trigger. As the minutes lengthened he recovered his breath.

"I lost my head then. If I lose it again, I won't make the grade."

The moon was rising as he finished filling in the grave. Panic was far behind. Even if the mastiff were to return, it would not know what had happened, and it would not attack him unprovoked. He carried the shotgun comfortably under his arm as he returned the spade to the shed.

Back in the cottage he shut the front door. In the kitchen he heated water on the oil stove, then stripped naked and washed in the zinc footbath. When he had dressed, he prepared supper. He poured a small whiskey, then put the bottle away. He would have to drive Crouch's car into London and leave it in a side street.

He did not bother to wash Crouch's glass. That kind of precaution was a waste of energy. His plan was based on the assumption that he could prevent suspicion from reaching him.

Shortly after midnight he was rested and ready to start. He took a light overcoat, knowing that he could not return until the day buses were running—even then he would have a four-mile walk.

Moonlight was bathing the marsh, glistening on the distant Thames, when he stepped out of the cottage. He shut the door behind him. There was no need to lock your doors in those parts.

At the same spot—by the tail of Crouch's car—came the same panic. He had stolen an oblique glance to the left, where the grave lay.

This time he saw the mastiff.

It was by the grave, sitting motionless on its haunches, guarding it as if it were guarding the car. The moonlight caught its eyes, which gleamed green.

Ignorant of the ways of a dog, Stretton thought it was unaware of his presence. He backed slowly, holding his breath, out of the line of vision. Then he bolted into the cottage for the shotgun—and spare cartridges.

The sporting gun, he knew, would be useless except at a range of a few feet. He would have to walk right up to the brute—or hold his fire to the last half-second if it attacked him. He crept out, telling himself that in less than a minute it would be all over—one way or the other.

The mastiff was in the same position. The same green glint came from the eyes. Within ten feet of it Stretton stopped. The mastiff took no notice of him. The luminous eyes were not looking at him. They were looking in the direction of the lane, as if expectantly.

Stretton advanced. The mastiff gave a low, indifferent growl—a protest rather than a menace. And still it would not look at him. It was positively ignoring him. Following a thought-pattern of its own?

But the mastiff's thought-pattern, if any, had never envisaged the nature of a gun . . .

The job of burying it would be even more laborious than that of burying its master. It would have to wait until he had rested. He managed to lever the carcass into a wheelbarrow and lurch with it into the garage. Then he had to go back to the cottage for another wash.

By half-past two he had dumped the car in Central London. He spent the rest of the night in a Turkish bath.

The next afternoon he buried the mastiff close to Crouch.

At midnight Mrs. Crouch, alarmed by the non-arrival of her husband at her father's house in Sussex, began to telephone inquiries as to road accidents. After ringing the vet and her own servants in Hampstead, she made a full report to Scotland Yard.

In the next few days the mastiff received its first installment of publicity—but only on the reasonable ground that it intensified the mystery of Crouch's disappearance.

No man, taking an illicit holiday with a fair companion, would burden himself with a mastiff. Nor could he lose his memory and disappear without being quickly identified by the presence of such a rare and noticeable animal. Any crook could shoot a mastiff: but to dispose of the carcass in a secret manner would be as difficult as to dispose of a corpse. The case became a murder mystery with, as it were, a double corpse.

For a week Stretton read the newspapers with anxiety. The schoolboy who had seen him getting into the car with Crouch had given a description which would fit tens of thousands. There were appeals to this unknown friend to communicate with the police. The lack of response created suspicion of the "big" man, but provided no clue to identity. No one east of London claimed to have seen a mastiff in a car. In a few days it became clear that there was nothing to lead the police to examine Stretton's garden.

Yet there were periods of depression and uncertainty, and some moments in which his scientific training and his common sense would again fail him. He felt no moral guilt, never gave a thought to Crouch as a person. But now and again his imagination was haunted by the luminous eyes of the mastiff staring expectantly in the direction of the lane—the mastiff that had a special affection for the police. There was that thought-pattern nonsense! Of course, some of the social insects—bees, ants, and whatnot— could achieve a sort of collective thinking—

"If dogs do have a thought-pattern of their own, they obviously can't communicate their conclusions to humanity—so what does it matter if they have!" Thus he would laugh it off: but he could never wholly forget it.

In a month of hard work the police failed to pick up any clue to the identity of the murderer or the whereabouts of the corpse, and the case was passed on to the Department of Dead Ends. Except when he lapsed into mysticism about the dog, Stretton lost the sense of peril.

The vision of Leonie's beauty no longer tormented him, so his nervous health improved. It was as if he were starting his life afresh, the past expiated and forgotten. In a couple of months he began preparations for a professional comeback.

He decided that he would have to live on in the cottage for a while. The potato patch bulged over the two graves. He finicked with a spade, breaking the outline. The soil might take a year or more to subside, he supposed, but while he remained at the cottage he was safe. The woman who did his housework had an elementary, incurious mind.

The woman came about eleven on Tuesdays, Thursdays, and Saturdays. By January he was driving to London on Mondays, Wednesdays, and Fridays to re-establish contacts in his practice as a consultant.

To put it in the absurd terms of Stretton's own mysticism, the mastiff spoke from the grave in the first week of February—some six months after the murder.

It was a little after ten on the Thursday morning. Stretton was rising late after a heavy evening on theory, and had just finished dressing when he saw a car draw up in the lane. Behind it was another—then a third and a fourth. Leisurely a dozen or more men emerged from the cars, some in police uniform.

Stretton hurried downstairs and opened the front door.

"Good Lord, sir, there he is!" exclaimed Detective Inspector Rason. "Cor! He'll ask us a lot of questions before we've dug up the answers. I thought he'd be in London by now."

"Your show!" said Superintendent Karslake grimly. As usual, he was in grave doubt as to the legality of Rason's position.

"Good morning, Mr. Stretton." Rason introduced himself and Karslake. "We have received certain information—that is—well, to cut it short, we'd like to do a spot of digging in your garden. Any objection?"

Stretton knew, of course, that he was done for, though there might still be some faint chance of stalling.

"That's a curious request," he said evenly. "I think I'm entitled to ask what sort of information?"

He expected them to say that they were looking for the body of Arthur Crouch. If they had said it, he would have kept his head.

"The information, Mr. Stretton," said Rason, "was furnished by a mastiff."

"My God!" gasped Stretton. As before, his hands sweated with superstitious terror, while his spine felt cold.

"Do I make myself clear, Mr. Stretton, or don't I?" chirped Rason. "I see that I do. Perhaps we can go inside and swap yarns while the men get busy. They won't be long. I was here yesterday with one of those young scientific farmers—you know, B.Sc. and all that! He spotted a patch over there where the earth had been dug up, he said, to a depth of several feet some time during the last year."

Stretton led them into the parlor. In half an hour, he supposed, the men would uncover the body. It would serve no purpose to pretend someone else had put it there. In those few steps all hope vanished. Dignity alone remained.

"I think you know already that your men will find the body of Arthur Crouch," he said.

"Steady on!" said Rason. "I have to warn you—"

"Unnecessary, thanks!" Stretton was taking it very well; but he lost some composure as he went on: "You implied that Crouch's mastiff is still alive. Either I'm partly mad, or your men will also dig up the carcass of that mastiff."

Rason gave him a long, noncommittal look.

"Are you *sure* that was the end of Arthur Crouch's mastiff, Mr. Stretton?"

Stretton's nerve gave. He gaped at the detective, then collapsed into the armchair.

"Are you telling me it was someone else's mastiff I killed?" The words came from the heart of a broken man.

"I've no statement to make, Mr. Stretton," replied Rason. "I'm sorry, but you'll have to work it out for yourself."

"It must have a natural explanation!" cried Stretton. "I *can* work it out. The million-to-one chance turned up. A second mastiff strayed into the garden. On that particular night! The million-to-one chance turned up!"

"And double the odds for luck," guffawed Rason.

"Even then, that thought-pattern rot turns out to be true!" Stretton's voice was slipping out of control. "And how the hell could that animal bring you here? It traveled on the floor of the car— six months ago! It's against reason, I tell you."

"Yet we are here!" said Rason.

A couple of hours later Rason was alone in a police car with Superintendent Karslake, on their way back to the Yard. Stretton had been taken away an hour previously in charge of a sergeant. Both smoked in silence until they were running into East London.

"Your case, and a good job o' work too, Rason!" Karslake's tone was aggrieved. "You've produced your evidence, and you don't have to tell me how you got it, if you don't want to."

Rason did not rise. Karslake continued: "Couldn't follow what he meant by a 'thought-pattern.' But he was right about that second mastiff being a million-to-one chance. It's the sort of thing that's turned up in your favor before."

"Yes, sir, only he was wrong," said Rason. "The whole point is that there is only one mastiff in this case. Actually there are only nine of 'em now in the whole country. I've made it my business to find out that not one of the nine has ever set foot in the county of Essex. All the same, I was speaking the truth when I told him a mastiff had furnished the information—"

"Wait a minute!" interrupted Karslake. "You told me last night, all formal and correct, that you had entered his cottage in his absence and taken fingerprints which corresponded to one set of prints found in Crouch's car. Also that you had taken along a soil expert, *et cetera*. But how did you find the cottage in the first place?"

"Oh, luck as usual!" Rason was inclined to be bitter on this point. But he relented at the other's disappointment. "You see, sir, my niece likes to do a bit o' shop-gazing—"

"Confound your niece!" exploded Karslake. "I'm sorry that slipped out, Rason. Nothing personal, of course! But it's not the first time you've stalled me with a wonderful fairy tale about that young lady. Can't we leave her out of it?"

"Okay!" grinned Rason. "To begin at the other end, have you ever seen a mastiff?"

"Y-yes. At a dog show some years ago. Awful looking brutes. Don't tell me your niece breeds 'em."

"No, she'd never seen one before." Rason was following his own train of thought. "And she was so tickled by what she did see that she went in and made inquiries. We might just as well go along ourselves." He leaned forward and spoke to the driver. "George, you can take us back via the Strand—and stop at No. 968."

The car stopped outside a shop which, in large lettering, proclaimed itself to be *The Dogs' Club*. The windows were partitioned into alcoves. In each alcove dogs were lounging.

Rason glanced at the windows.

"It's gone!" he exclaimed ruefully. "Maybe it's inside."

In the shop Rason nodded to an assistant and pressed on to the proprietor's office at the rear.

"Mr. Braddell, this is my senior, Superintendent Karslake. Could you show him what you showed my niece—and tell him what you told me?"

"Certainly. We've had an offer for the dog and he'll probably be gone tomorrow—unless the Yard wants him?"

"No, thanks! He's done his job for us."

Mr. Braddell took them into a long room tiered with cages containing dogs of almost every known breed.

"There you are, Mr. Karslake!"

"Where?" asked Karslake. He was looking for a mastiff.

Rason pointed to a medium-sized dog with a white shaggy coat and a somewhat astonishing head.

"What is that animal?" asked Karslake.

"Pure cross-breed—sheepdog and mastiff," answered Mr. Braddell.

"You see, sir?" cut in Rason. "Sheep dog—mastiff! Mastiff—sheepdog! That's the thought-pattern you want!"

"The puppies," said Mr. Braddell, "were brought to us by a small farmer in Essex, near the marshes. He didn't know what they were. Nor did we—until the mastiff head began to develop."

"My niece," said Rason, "saw two of 'em in the window. Happened to mention it to me over tea."

From the 1951 anthology . . .

Perhaps the most brilliant writer of crime short stories to emerge in this country since World War II is Stanley Ellin, who since the appearance of his prize-winning "The Specialty of the House" in 1945 has heaped success upon success. I wholeheartedly recommend tracking down Mr. Ellin's two collections of short stories, Mystery Stories (1956) and The Blessington Method and Other Strange Tales (1964). In the meantime, have a chilling glimpse into . . .

STANLEY ELLIN

The Orderly World of Mr. Appleby

Mr. Appleby was a small, prim man who wore rimless spectacles, parted his graying hair in the middle, and took sober pleasure in pointing out that there was no room in the properly organized life for the operations of Chance. Consequently, when he decided that the time had come to investigate the most efficient methods for disposing of his wife he knew where to look.

He found the book, a text on forensic medicine, on the shelf of a second-hand bookshop among several volumes of like topic, and since all but one were in a distressingly shabby and dog-eared state which offended him to his very core, he chose the only one in reasonably good condition. Most of the cases it presented, he discovered on closer examination, were horrid studies of the results (vividly illustrated) of madness and lust—enough to set any decent man wondering at the number of monsters inhabiting the earth. One case, however, seemed to be exactly what he was looking for, and this he made the object of his most intensive study.

It was the case of Mrs. X (the book was replete with Mrs. X's, and Mr. Y's, and Miss Z's) who died after what was presumably an accidental fall on a scatter rug in her home. However, a lawyer representing the interests of the late lamented charged her husband with murder, and at a coroner's investigation was attempting to prove his charge when the accused abruptly settled matters by dropping dead of a heart attack.

All this was of moderate interest to Mr. Appleby whose motive, a desire to come into the immediate possession of his wife's estate, was strikingly similar to the alleged motive of Mrs. X's husband. But more important were the actual details of the case. Mrs. X had been in the act of bringing him a glass of water, said her husband, when the scatter rug, as scatter rugs will, had suddenly slipped from under her feet.

In rebuttal the indefatigable lawyer had produced a medical authority who made clear through a number of charts (all of which were handsomely reproduced in the book) that in the act of receiving the glass of water it would have been child's-play for the husband to lay one hand behind his wife's shoulder, another hand along her jaw, and with a sudden thrust produce the same drastic results as the fall on the scatter rug, without leaving any clues as to the nature of his crime.

It should be made clear now that in studying these charts and explanations relentlessly Mr. Appleby was not acting the part of the greedy man going to any lengths to appease that greed. True, it was money he wanted, but it was money for the maintenance of what he regarded as a holy cause. And that was the Shop: *Appleby, Antiques and Curios.*

The Shop was the sun of Mr. Appleby's universe. He had bought it twenty years before with the pittance left by his father, and at best it provided him with a poor living. At worst—and it was usually at worst—it had forced him to draw on his mother's meagre store of good will and capital. Since his mother was not one to give up a penny lightly, the Shop brought about a series of pitched battles which, however, always saw it the victor—since in the last analysis the Shop was to Mr. Appleby what Mr. Appleby was to his mother.

This unhappy triangle was finally shattered by his mother's death, at which time Mr. Appleby discovered that she had played a far greater role in maintaining his orderly little world than he had hitherto realized. This concerned not only the money she occasionally gave him, but also his personal habits.

He ate lightly and warily. His mother had been adept at toasting and boiling his meals to perfection. His nerves were violently shaken if anything in the house was out of place, and she had been a living assurance he would be spared this. Her death, therefore, left a vast and uncomfortable gap in his life, and in studying methods to fill it he was led to contemplate marriage, and then to the act itself.

His wife was a pale, thin-lipped woman so much like his mother in appearance and gesture that sometimes on her entrance into a room he was taken aback by the resemblance. In only one respect did she fail him: she could not understand the significance of the Shop, nor his feelings about it. That was disclosed the first time he broached the subject of a small loan that would enable him to meet some business expenses.

Mrs. Appleby had been well in the process of withering on the vine when her husband-to-be had proposed to her, but to give her full due she was not won by the mere prospect of finally making a marriage. Actually, though she would have blushed at such a blunt statement of her secret thought, it was the large mournful eyes behind his rimless spectacles that turned the trick, promising, as they did, hidden depths of emotion neatly garbed in utter respectability. When she learned very soon after her wedding that the hidden depths were evidently too well hidden ever to be explored by her, she shrugged the matter off and turned to boiling and toasting his meals with good enough grace. The knowledge that the impressive *Appleby, Antiques and Curios* was a hollow shell she took in a different spirit.

She made some brisk investigations and then announced her findings to Mr. Appleby with some heat.

"Antiques and curios!" she said shrilly. "Why, that whole collection of stuff is nothing but a pile of junk. Just a bunch of worthless dust-catchers, that's all it is!"

What she did not understand was that these objects, which to the crass and commercial eye might seem worthless, were to Mr. Appleby the stuff of life itself. The Shop had grown directly from his childhood mania for collecting, assorting, labeling, and preserving anything he could lay his hands on. And the value of any item in the Shop increased proportionately with the length of time he possessed it; whether a cracked imitation of Sèvres, or clumsily faked Chippendale, or rusty sabre made no difference. Each piece had won a place for itself; a permanent, immutable place, as far as Mr. Appleby was concerned; and strangely enough it was the sincere agony he suffered in giving up a piece that led to the few sales he made. The customer who was uncertain of values had only to get a glimpse of this agony to be convinced that he was getting a rare bargain. Fortunately, no customer could have imagined for a moment that it was the thought of the empty space left by the object's departure—the brief disorder which the emptiness made—and not a passion for the object itself that drew Mr. Appleby's pinched features into a mask of pain.

So, not understanding, Mrs. Appleby took an unsympathetic tack. "You'll get my mite when I'm dead and gone," she said, "and only when I'm dead and gone."

Thus unwittingly she tried herself, was found wanting, and it only remained for sentence to be executed. When the time came Mr. Appleby applied the lessons he had gleaned from his invaluable textbook and found them accurate in every detail. It was over quickly, quietly, and, outside of a splash of water on his trousers, neatly. The Medical Examiner growled something about those indescribable scatter rugs costing more lives than drunken motorists; the policeman in charge kindly offered to do whatever he could in the way of making funeral arrangements; and that was all there was to it.

It had been so easy—so undramatic, in fact—that it was not until a week later when a properly sympathetic lawyer was making him an accounting of his wife's estate that Mr. Appleby suddenly understood the whole, magnificent new world that had been opened up to him.

Discretion must sometimes outweigh sentiment, and Mr. Appleby was, if anything, a discreet man. After his wife's estate had been cleared, the Shop was moved to another location far from it's original setting. It was moved again after the sudden demise of the second Mrs. Appleby, and by the time the sixth Mrs. Appleby had been disposed of, the removals were merely part of a fruitful pattern.

Because of their similarities—they were all pale, thin-featured women with pinched lips, adept at toasting and boiling, and adamant on the subjects of regularity and order—Mr. Appleby was inclined to remember his departed wives rather vaguely *en masse*. Only in one regard did he qualify them: the number of digits their bank accounts totaled up to. For that reason he thought of the first two Mrs. Applebys as Fours; the third as a Three (an unpleasant surprise); and the last three as Fives. The sum would have been a pretty penny by anyone else's standards, but since each succeeding portion of it had been snapped up by the insatiable *Appleby, Antiques and Curios*—in much the way a fly is snapped up by a hungry lizard—Mr. Appleby found himself soon after the burial of the sixth Mrs. Appleby in deeper and warmer financial waters than ever. So desperate were his circumstances that although he dreamed of another Five he would have settled for a Four on the spot. It was at this opportune moment that Martha Sturgis entered his life, and after fifteen minutes conversation with her he brushed all thoughts of Fours and Fives from his mind.

Martha Sturgis, it seemed, was a Six.

It was not only in the extent of her fortune that she broke the pattern established by the women of Mr. Appleby's previous experience. Unlike them, Martha Sturgis was a large, rather shapeless woman who in person, dress, and manner might almost be called (Mr. Appleby shuddered a little at the word) blowzy.

It was remotely possible that properly veneered, harnessed, coiffured, and appareled she might have been made into something presentable, but from all indications Martha Sturgis was a woman who went out of her way to defy such conventions. Her hair, dyed a shocking orange-red, was piled carelessly on her head; her blobby features were recklessly powdered and painted entirely to their disadvantage; her clothes, obviously worn for comfort, were, at the same time, painfully garish; and her shoes gave evidence of long and pleasurable wear without corresponding care being given their upkeep.

Of all this and its effect on the beholder Martha Sturgis seemed totally unaware. She strode through *Appleby, Antiques and Curios* with an energy that set movable objects dancing in their places; she smoked incessantly, lighting one cigarette from another, while Mr. Appleby fanned the air before his face and coughed suggestively; and she talked without pause, loudly and in a deep, hoarse voice that dinned strangely in a Shop so accustomed to the higher, thinner note.

In the first fourteen minutes of their acquaintance the one quality she displayed that led Mr. Appleby to modify some of his immediate revulsion even a trifle was the care with which she priced each article. She examined, evaluated, and cross-examined in detail before moving on with obvious disapproval, and he moved along with her with mounting assurance that he could get her out of the Shop before any damage was done to the stock or his patience. And then in the fifteenth minute she spoke the Word.

"I've got half a million dollars in the bank," Martha Sturgis remarked with cheerful contempt, "but I never thought I'd get around to spending a nickel of it on this kind of stuff."

Mr. Appleby had his hand before his face preparatory to waving aside some of the tobacco smoke that eddied about him. In the time it took the hand to drop nervelessly to his side his mind attacked an astonishing number of problems. One concerned the important finger on her left hand which was ringless; the others concerned certain mathematical problems largely dealing with short-term notes, long-term notes, and rates of interest. By the time the hand touched his side, the problems, as far as Mr. Appleby was concerned, were well on the way to solution.

And it may be noted there was an added fillip given the matter by the very nature of Martha Sturgis's slovenly and strident being. Looking at her after she had spoken the Word, another man might perhaps have seen her through the sort of veil that a wise photographer casts over the lens of his camera in taking the picture of a prosperous, but unprepossessing, subject. Mr. Appleby, incapable of such self-deceit, girded himself instead with the example of the man who carried a heavy weight on his back for the pleasure it gave him in laying it down. Not only would the final act of a marriage to Martha Sturgis solve important mathematical problems, but it was an act he could play out with the gusto of a man ridding the world of an unpleasant object.

Therefore he turned his eyes, more melancholy and luminous than ever, on her and said, "It's a great pity, Mrs. . . ."

She told him her name, emphasizing the Miss before it, and Mr Appleby smiled apologetically.

"Of course. As I was saying, it's a great pity when someone o refinement and culture—" (the like yourself floated delicately unsaid on the air) "—should never have known the joy in possession of fine works of art. But, as we all learn, it is never too late to begin, is it?"

Martha Sturgis looked at him sharply and then laughed a hearty bellow of laughter that stabbed his eardrums painfully. For a moment Mr. Appleby, a man not much given to humor, wondered darkly if he had unwittingly uttered something so excruciatingly epigrammatic that it was bound to have this alarming effect.

"My dear man," said Martha Sturgis, "if it is your idea that I am here to start cluttering up my life with your monstrosities, perish the thought. What I'm here for is to buy a gift for a friend, a thoroughly infuriating and loathesome person who happens to have the nature and disposition of a bar of stainless steel. I can't think of a better way of showing my feelings toward her than by presenting her with almost anything displayed in your shop. If possible, I should also like delivery arranged so that I can be on the scene when she receives the package."

Mr. Appleby staggered under this, then rallied valiantly. "In that case," he said, and shook his head firmly, "it is out of the question. Completely out of the question."

"Nonsense," Martha Sturgis said. "I'll arrange for delivery myself if you can't handle it. Really, you ought to understand that there's no point in doing this sort of thing unless you're on hand to watch the results."

Mr. Appleby kept tight rein on his temper. "I am not alluding to the matter of delivery," he said. "What I am trying to make clear is that I cannot possibly permit anything in my Shop to be bought in such a spirit. Not for any price you could name."

Martha Sturgis's heavy jaw dropped. "What was that you said?" she asked blankly.

It was a perilous moment, and Mr. Appleby knew it. His next words could set her off into another spasm of that awful laughter that would devastate him completely; or, worse, could send her right out of the Shop forever; or could decide the issue in his favor then and there. But it was a moment that had to be met, and, thought Mr. Appleby desperately, whatever else Martha Sturgis might be, she was a Woman.

He took a deep breath. "It is the policy of this Shop," he said quietly, "never to sell anything unless the prospective purchaser shows full appreciation for the article to be bought and can assure it the care and devotion to which it is entitled. That has always been the policy, and always will be as long as I am here. Anything other than that I would regard as desecration."

He watched Martha Sturgis with bated breath. There was a chair nearby, and she dropped into it heavily so that her skirts were drawn tight by her widespread thighs, and the obscene shoes were displayed mercilessly. She lit another cigarette, regarding him meanwhile with narrowed eyes through the flame of the match, and then fanned the air a little to dispel the cloud of smoke.

"You know," she said, "this is very interesting. I'd like to hear more about it."

To the inexperienced the problem of drawing information of the most personal nature from a total stranger would seem a perplexing one. To Mr. Appleby, whose interests had so often been dependent on such information, it was no problem at all. In very short time he had evidence that Martha Sturgis's estimate of her fortune was quite accurate, that she was apparently alone in the world without relatives or intimate friends, and—that she was not averse to the idea of marriage.

This last he drew from her during her now regular visits to the Shop where she would spread herself comfortably on a chair and talk to him endlessly. Much of her talk was about her father to whom Mr. Appleby evidently bore a striking resemblance.

"He even dressed like you," Martha Sturgis said reflectively. "Neat as a pin, and not only about himself either. He used to make an inspection of the house every day—march through and make sure everything was exactly where it had to be. And he kept it up right to the end. I remember an hour before he died how he went about straightening pictures on the wall."

Mr. Appleby who had been peering with some irritation at a picture that hung slightly awry on the Shop wall turned his attentions reluctantly from it.

"And you were with him to the end?" he asked sympathetically.

"Indeed I was."

"Well," Mr. Appleby said brightly, "One does deserve some reward for such sacrifice, doesn't one? Especially—and I hope this will not embarrass you, Miss Sturgis—when one considers that such a woman as yourself could undoubtedly have left the care o an aged father to enter matrimony almost at will. Isn't that so?"

Martha Sturgis sighed. "Maybe it is, and maybe it isn't," she said, "and I won't deny that I've had my dreams. But that's all they are, and I suppose that's all they ever will be."

"Why?" asked Mr. Appleby encouragingly.

"Because," said Martha Sturgis sombrely, "I have never yet met the man who could fit those dreams. I am not a simpering school-girl, Mr. Appleby; I don't have to balance myself against my bank account to know why any man would devote himself to me, and frankly, his motives would be of no interest. But he must be a decent, respectable man who would spend every moment of his life worrying about me and caring for me; and he must be a man who would make the memory of my father a living thing."

Mr. Appleby rested a hand lightly on her shoulder.

"Miss Sturgis," he said gravely, "You may yet meet such a man."

She looked at him with features that were made even more blobby and unattractive by her emotion.

"Do you mean that, Mr. Appleby?" she asked. "Do you really believe that?"

Faith glowed in Mr. Appleby's eyes as he smiled down at her. "He may be closer than you dare realize," he said warmly.

Experience had proved to Mr. Appleby that once the ice is broken the best thing to do is take a deep breath and plunge in. Accordingly, he let very few days elapse before he made his proposal.

"Miss Sturgis," he said, "there comes a time to every lonely man when he can no longer bear his loneliness. If at such a time he is fortunate enough to meet the one woman to whom he could give unreservedly all his respect and tender feelings, he is a fortunate man indeed. Miss Sturgis—I am that man."

"Why, Mr. Appleby!" said Martha Sturgis, coloring a trifle. "That's really very good of you, but . . ."

At this note of indecision his heart sank. "Wait!" he interposed hastily. "If you have any doubts, Miss Sturgis, please speak them now so that I may answer them. Considering the state of my emotions, that would only be fair, wouldn't it?"

"Well, I suppose so," said Martha Sturgis. "You see, Mr. Appleby, I'd rather not get married at all than take the chance of getting someone who wasn't prepared to give me exactly what I'm looking for in marriage: absolute, single-minded devotion all the rest of my days."

"Miss Sturgis," said Mr. Appleby solemnly, "I am prepared to give you no less."

"Men say these things so easily," she sighed. "But—I shall certainly think about it, Mr. Appleby."

The dismal prospect of waiting an indefinite time for a woman of such careless habits to render a decision was not made any lighter by the sudden receipt a few days later of a note peremptorily requesting Mr. Appleby's presence at the offices of Gainsborough, Gainsborough, and Golding, attorneys-at-law. With his creditors closing in like a wolf pack, Mr. Appleby could only surmise the worst, and he was pleasantly surprised upon his arrival at Gainsborough, Gainsborough, and Golding to find that they represented, not his creditors, but Martha Sturgis herself.

The elder Gainsborough, obviously very much the guiding spirit of the firm, was a short, immensely fat man with pendulous dewlaps that almost concealed his collar, and large fishy eyes that goggled at Mr. Appleby. The younger Gainsborough was a duplicate of his brother with jowls not quite so impressive, while Golding was an impassive young man with a hatchet face.

"This," said the elder Gainsborough, his eyes fixed glassily on Mr. Appleby, "is a delicate matter. Miss Sturgis, an esteemed client—" the younger Gainsborough nodded at this "—has mentioned entering matrimony with you, sir."

Mr. Appleby sitting primly on his chair was stirred by a pleased excitement. "Yes?" he said.

"And," continued the elder Gainsborough, "while Miss Sturgis is perfectly willing to concede that her fortune may be the object of attraction in any suitor's eyes—" he held up a pudgy hand to cut short Mr. Appleby's shocked protest "—she is also willing to dismiss that issue—"

"To ignore it, set it aside," said the younger Gainsborough sternly.

"—if the suitor is prepared to meet all other expectations in marriage."

"I am," said Mr. Appleby fervently.

"Mr. Appleby," said the elder Gainsborough abruptly, "have you been married before?"

Mr. Appleby thought swiftly. Denial would make any chance word about his past a deadly trap; admission, on the other hand, was a safeguard against that, and a thoroughly respectable one.

"Yes," he said.

"Divorced?"

"Good heavens, no!" said Mr. Appleby, genuinely shocked.

The Gainsboroughs looked at each other in approval. "Good," said the elder; "very good. Perhaps, Mr. Appleby, the question seemed impertinent, but in these days of moral laxity . . ."

"I should like it known in that case," said Mr. Appleby sturdily, "that I am as far from moral laxity as any human being can be. Tobacco, strong drink, and—ah—"

"Loose women," said the younger Gainsborough briskly.

"Yes," said Mr. Appleby reddening; "are unknown to me."

The elder Gainsborough nodded. "Under any conditions," he said, "Miss Sturgis will not make any precipitate decision. She should have her answer for you within a month, however, and during that time, if you don't mind taking the advice of an old man, I suggest that you court her assiduously. She is a woman, Mr. Appleby, and I imagine that all women are much alike."

"I imagine they are," said Mr. Appleby.

"Devotion," said the younger Gainsborough. "Constancy. That's the ticket."

What he was being asked to do, Mr. Appleby reflected in one of his solitary moments, was to put aside the Shop and the orderly world it represented and to set the unappealing figure of Martha Sturgis in its place. It was a temporary measure, of course; it was one that would prove richly rewarding when Martha Sturgis had been properly wed and sent the way of the preceding Mrs. Applebys; but it was not made any easier by enforced familiarity with the woman. It was inevitable that since Mr. Appleby viewed matters not only as a prospective bridegroom, but also as a prospective widower, so to speak, he found his teeth constantly set on edge by the unwitting irony which crept into so many of her tedious discussions on marriage.

"The way I see it," Martha Sturgis once remarked, "is that a man who would divorce his wife would divorce any other woman he ever married. You take a look at all these broken marriages today, and I'll bet that in practically every case you'll find a man who's always shopping around and never finding what he wants.

Now, the man I marry," she said pointedly, "must be willing to settle down and stay settled."

"Of course," said Mr. Appleby.

"I have heard," Martha Sturgis told him on another, and particularly trying, occasion, "that a satisfactory marriage increases a woman's span of years. That's an excellent argument for marriage, don't you think?"

"Of course," said Mr. Appleby.

It seemed to him that during that month of trial most of his conversation was restricted to the single phrase "of course," delivered with varying inflections; but the tactic must have been the proper one since at the end of the month he was able to change the formula to "I do," in a wedding ceremony at which Gainsborough, Gainsborough, and Golding were the sole guests.

Immediately afterward, Mr. Appleby (to his discomfort) was borne off with his bride to a photographer's shop where innumerable pictures were made under the supervision of the dour Golding, following which, Mr. Appleby (to his delight) exchanged documents with his wife which made them each other's heirs to all properties, possessions, et cetera, whatsoever.

If Mr. Appleby had occasionally appeared rather abstracted during these festivities, it was only because his mind was neatly arranging the program of impending events. The rug (the very same one that had served so well in six previous episodes) had to be placed; and then there would come the moment when he would ask for a glass of water, when he would place one hand on her shoulder, and with the other. . . . It could not be a moment that took place without due time passing; yet it could not be forestalled too long in view of the pressure exercised by the Shop's voracious creditors. Watching the pen in his wife's hand as she signed her will, he decided there would be time within a few weeks. With the will in his possession there would be no point in waiting longer than that.

Before the first of those weeks was up, however, Mr. Appleby knew that even this estimate would have to undergo drastic revision. There was no question about it: he was simply not equipped to cope with his marriage.

For one thing, her home (and now his), a brownstone cavern inherited from her mother, was a nightmare of disorder. On the principle, perhaps, that anything flung casually aside was not worth picking up since it would only be flung aside again, an amazing litter had accumulated in every room. The contents of brimming closets and drawers were recklessly exchanged, mislaid, or added to the general litter, and over all lay a thin film of dust. On Mr. Appleby's quivering nervous system all this had the effect of a fingernail dragging along an endless blackboard.

The one task to which Mrs. Appleby devoted herself, as it happened, was the one which her husband prayerfully wished she would spare herself. She doted on cookery, and during mealtimes would trudge back and forth endlessly between kitchen and dining room laden with dishes outside any of Mr. Appleby's experience.

At his first feeble protests his wife had taken pains to explain in precise terms that she was sensitive to any criticism of her cooking, even the implied criticism of a partly emptied plate; and, thereafter, Mr. Appleby, plunging hopelessly through rare meats, rich sauces, and heavy pastries, found added to his tribulations the incessant pangs of dyspepsia. Nor were his pains eased by his wife's insistence that he prove himself a trencherman of her mettle. She would thrust plates heaped high with indigestibles under his quivering nose, and, bracing himself like a martyr facing the lions, Mr. Appleby would empty his portion into a digestive tract that cried for simple fare properly boiled or toasted.

It became one of his fondest waking dreams, that scene where he returned from his wife's burial to dine on hot tea and toast and, perhaps, a medium-boiled egg. But even that dream and its sequel —where he proceeded to set the house in order—were not sufficient to buoy him up each day when he awoke and reflected on what lay ahead of him.

Each day found his wife more insistent in her demands for his attentions. And on that day when she openly reproved him for devoting more of those attentions to the Shop than to herself, Mr. Appleby knew the time had come to prepare for the final act. He brought home the rug that evening and carefully laid it in place between the living room and the hallway that led to the kitchen. Martha Appleby watched him without any great enthusiasm.

"That's a shabby looking thing, all right," she said. "What is it, Appie, an antique or something?"

She had taken to calling him by that atrocious name and seemed cheerfully oblivious to the way he winced under it. He winced now.

"It is not an antique," Mr. Appleby admitted, "but I hold it dear for many reasons. It has a great deal of sentimental value to me."

Mrs. Appleby smiled fondly at him. "And you brought it for me, didn't you?"

"Yes," said Mr. Appleby, "I did."

"You're a dear," said Mrs. Appleby. "You really are."

Watching her cross the rug on slip-shod feet to use the telephone, which stood on a small table the other side of the hallway, Mr. Appleby toyed with the idea that since she used the telephone at about the same time every evening he could schedule the accident for that time. The advantages were obvious: since those calls seemed to be the only routine she observed with any fidelity, she would cross the rug at a certain time, and he would be in a position to settle matters then and there.

However, thought Mr. Appleby as he polished his spectacles, that brought up the problem of how best to approach her under such circumstances. Clearly the tried and tested methods were best, but if the telephone call and the glass of water could be synchronized . . .

"A penny for your thoughts, Appie," said Mrs. Appleby brightly. She had laid down the telephone and crossed the hallway so that she stood squarely on the rug. Mr. Appleby replaced his spectacles and peered at her through them.

"I wish," he said querulously, "you would not address me by that horrid name. You know I detest it."

"Nonsense," his wife said briefly. "I think it's cute."

"I do not."

"Well, I like it," said Mrs. Appleby with the air of one who has settled a matter once and for all. "Anyhow," she pouted, "That couldn't have been what you were thinking about before I started talking to you, could it?"

It struck Mr. Appleby that when this stout, unkempt woman pouted, she resembled nothing so much as a wax doll badly worn by time and handling. He pushed away the thought to frame some suitable answer.

"As it happens," he said, "my mind was on the disgraceful state of my clothes. Need I remind you again that there are buttons missing from practically every garment I own?"

Mrs. Appleby yawned broadly. "I'll get to it sooner or later."

"Tomorrow perhaps?"

"I doubt it," said Mrs. Appleby. She turned toward the stairs. "Come to sleep, Appie. I'm dead tired."

Mr. Appleby followed her thoughtfully. Tomorrow, he knew, he would have to get one of his suits to the tailor if he wanted to have anything fit to wear at the funeral.

He had brought home the suit and hung it neatly away; he had eaten his dinner; and he had sat in the living room listening to his wife's hoarse voice go on for what seemed interminable hours, although the clock was not yet at nine.

Now with rising excitement he saw her lift herself slowly from her chair and cross the room to the hallway. As she reached for the telephone Mr. Appleby cleared his throat sharply. "If you don't mind," he said, "I'd like a glass of water."

Mrs. Appleby turned to look at him. "A glass of water?"

"If you don't mind," said Mr. Appleby, and waited as she hesitated, then set down the telephone, and turned toward the kitchen. There was the sound of a glass being rinsed in the kitchen, and then Mrs. Appleby came up to him holding it out. He laid one hand appreciatively on her plump shoulder, and then lifted the other as if to brush back a strand of untidy hair at her cheek.

"Is that what happened to all the others?" said Mrs. Appleby quietly.

Mr. Appleby felt his hand freeze in mid-air and the chill from it run down into his marrow. "Others?" he managed to say. "What others?"

His wife smiled grimly at him, and he saw that the glass of water in her hand was perfectly steady. "Six others," she said. "That is, six by my count. Why? Were there any more?"

"No," he said, then caught wildly at himself. "I don't understand what you're talking about!"

"Dear Appie. Surely you couldn't forget six wives just like that. Unless, of course, I've come to mean so much to you that you can't bear to think of the others. That would be a lovely thing to happen, wouldn't it?"

"I was married before," Mr. Appleby said loudly. "I made that quite clear myself. But this talk about six wives!"

"Of course you were married before, Appie. And it was quite easy to find out to whom—and it was just as easy to find out about the one before that—and all the others. Or even about your mother, or where you went to school, or where you were born. You see, Appie, Mr. Gainsborough is really a very clever man."

"Then it was Gainsborough who put you up to this!"

"Not at all, you foolish little man," his wife said contemptuously. "All the time you were making your plans I was unmaking them. From the moment I laid eyes on you I knew you for what you are. Does that surprise you?"

Mr. Appleby struggled with the emotions of a man who had picked up a twig to find a viper in his hand. "How could you know?" he gasped.

"Because you were the image of my father. Because in everything—the way you dress, your insufferable neatness, your priggish arrogance, the little moral lectures you dote on—you are what he was. And all my life I hated him for what he was, and what it did to my mother. He married her for her money, made her every day a nightmare, and then killed her for what was left of her fortune."

"Killed her?" said Mr. Appleby, stupefied.

"Oh, come," his wife said sharply. "Do you think you're the only man who was ever capable of that? Yes, he killed her— murdered her, if you prefer—by asking for a glass of water, and then breaking her neck when she offered it to him. A method strangely similar to yours, isn't it?"

Mr. Appleby found the incredible answer rising to his mind, but refused to accept it. "What happened to him?" he demanded. "Tell me, what happened! Was he caught?"

"No, he was never caught. There were no witnesses to what he did, but Mr. Gainsborough had been my mother's lawyer, a dear friend of hers. He had suspicions and demanded a hearing. He brought a doctor to the hearing who made it plain how my father could have killed her and made it look as if she had slipped on a rug, but before there was any decision my father died of a heart attack."

"That was the case—the case I read!" Mr. Appleby groaned, and then was silent under his wife's sardonic regard.

"When he was gone," she went on inexorably, "I swore I would some day find a man exactly like that, and I would make that man live the life my father should have lived. I would know his every habit and every taste, and none of them should go satisfied. I would know he married me for my money, and he would never get a penny of it until I was dead and gone. And that would be a long, long time, because he would spend his life taking care that I should live out my life to the last possible breath."

Mr. Appleby pulled his wits together, and saw that despite her emotion she had remained in the same position. "How can you make him do that?" he asked softly, and moved an inch closer.

"It does sound strange, doesn't it, Appie?" she observed. "But hardly as strange as the fact that your six wives died by slipping on a rug—very much like this one—while bringing you a glass of water—very much like this one. So strange, that Mr. Gainsborough was led to remark that too many coincidences will certainly hang a man. Especially if there is reason to bring them to light in a trial for murder."

Mr. Appleby suddenly found the constriction of his collar unbearable. "That doesn't answer my question," he said craftily. "How can you make sure that I would devote my life to prolonging yours?"

"A man whose wife is in a position to have him hanged should be able to see that clearly."

"No," said Mr. Appleby in a stifled voice, "I only see that such a man is forced to rid himself of his wife as quickly as possible."

"Ah, but that's where the arrangements come in."

"Arrangements? What arrangements?" demanded Mr. Appleby.

"I'd like very much to explain them," his wife said. "In fact, I see the time has come when it's imperative to do so. But I do find it uncomfortable standing here like this."

"Never mind that," said Mr. Appleby impatiently, and his wife shrugged.

"Well, then," she said coolly, "Mr. Gainsborough now has all the documents about your marriages—the way the previous deaths took place, the way you always happened to get the bequests at just the right moment to pay your shop's debts.

"Besides this, he has a letter from me, explaining that in the event of my death an investigation be made immediately and all necessary action be taken. Mr. Gainsborough is really very efficient. The fingerprints and photographs . . ."

"Fingerprints and photographs!" cried Mr. Appleby.

"Of course. After my father's death it was found that he had made all preparations for a quick trip abroad. Mr. Gainsborough has assured me that in case you had such ideas in mind you should get rid of them. No matter where you are, he said, it will be quite easy to bring you back again."

"What do you want of me?" asked Mr. Appleby numbly. "Surely you don't expect me to stay now, and—"

"Oh, yes, I do. And since we've come to this point I may as well tell you I expect you to give up your useless shop once and for all, and make it a point to be at home with me the entire day."

"Give up the Shop!" he exclaimed.

"You must remember, Appie, that in my letter asking for a full investigation at my death, I did not specify death by any particular means. I look forward to a long and pleasant life with you always at my side, and perhaps—mind you, I only say perhaps—some day I shall turn over that letter and all the evidence to you. You can see how much it is to your interest, therefore, to watch over me very carefully."

The telephone rang with abrupt violence, and Mrs. Appleby nodded toward it. "Almost as carefully," she said softly, "as Mr. Gainsborough. Unless I call him every evening at nine to report I am well and happy, it seems he will jump to the most shocking conclusions."

"Wait," said Mr. Appleby. He lifted the telephone, and there was no mistaking the voice that spoke.

"Hello," said the elder Gainsborough. "Hello, Mrs. Appleby?"

Mr. Appleby essayed a cunning move. "No," he said, "I'm afraid she can't speak to you now. What is it?"

The voice in his ear took on an unmistakable cold menace. "This is Gainsborough, Mr. Appleby, and I wish to speak to your wife immediately. I will give you ten seconds to have her at this telephone, Mr. Appleby. Do you understand?"

Mr. Appleby turned dully toward his wife and held out the telephone. "It's for you," he said, and then saw with a start of terror that as she turned to set down the glass of water the rug skidded slightly under her feet. Her arms flailed the air as she fought for balance, the glass smashed at his feet drenching his neat trousers, and her face twisted into a silent scream. Then her body struck the floor and lay inertly in the position with which he was so familiar.

Watching her, he was barely conscious of the voice emerging tinnily from the telephone in his hand.

"The ten seconds are up, Mr. Appleby," it said shrilly. "Do you understand? *Your time is up!*"

Few of the stories in the Best Detective *series are tales of terror, but "Total Recall" from the 1952 anthology will more than adequately represent those that are. The circumstances are almost archetypal: honeymooners alone on the desolate moors, threatened by a homicidal maniac. But so effectively is mood communicated, so starkly is the climax painted, that here is shattering reading indeed.*

JAMES HELVICK

Total Recall

On the kitchen floor of the moorland cottage, pushed in through the wide crack under the door, they found two letters. One was a threat of death. The other was an offer of help. Both letters must have been slid under the locked door during the five hours the Mansells had been out on the moor. The offer lay nearer to the door than the threat, as though it had been pushed there later.

Edward Mansell read the offer first, and his look of vague boredom became one of bewilderment. Then he read the threat. Joan Mansell, looking on irritably, saw him reach out and close the door without taking his eyes from the letter. When he started to read the first letter again, she snapped impatiently, "Oh, what is it? What is it then?"

This holiday on the moor was to have been a kind of second honeymoon after a year of marriage. And today they had spent five hours walking, picnicking, and wrangling about everything or nothing. They'd got on each other's nerves all day; their relations seemed to be at the breaking point, and Edward chose this moment to stand there reading these letters as though she were not there.

He touched her shoulder gently. "What?" she said.

He said, "Well, this. You'd better have a look." He gave her the letters, and she stood reading them in the same order that he had. The first said:

> Dear Mr. Mansell: I hope you won't consider this an impertinence from a total stranger, but in view of the news about the man Howard being at large somewhere in these parts, I thought, as your place is so very isolated, you might be glad of a little reinforcement. I don't suppose he'll come anywhere near you, but still, he is supposed to be a very dangerous maniac, and I took the liberty of suggesting to the police at Buckforth that they ought to post a man with you tonight. But they are so busy with their "Man hunts" and "Cordons" that it seems they just haven't anybody to spare. So it occurred to me that, as I shall in any case be cycling to the "outer edge" of the parish late this afternoon, I might look in on you on the way back and, if you think it would be a good idea, I could help you do sentry go during the night. Probably quite unnecessary, as the police think Howard is over on the other side of moor by now. But in any case, I should be very glad to make your acquaintance, and hope you will not, under the circumstances, think me intrusive.

It was signed: *George Beale,* with *Curate at Buckforth (in case you didn't know!)* after the signature.

The other letter was written on expensive paper, in an elegant hand, covering four rather large pages. It opened with a detailed and obscenely worded threat to torture and murder the inhabitants of that cottage during the night. The rest of the letter was a series of reiterations and elaborations of the threat. It was signed "Barrington Howard."

It took a long moment for the meaning of the letter to drive the irritated expression from Joan Mansell's face, leaving it momentarily blank. Then she swung round to Edward, touching the tweed of his sleeve with her fingertips.

"But, Eddie—all this—it's crazy, isn't it?"

He frowned, taking the letters from her. "Well," he said, "I suppose—" His eyes turned toward the low window of the kitchen, beyond which lay the moor. She noticed his glance and jerked round abruptly, staring toward the window, her hand to her mouth.

"You mean," she gasped, "there's really something—someone, I mean—out there?"

"Probably nowhere near here. Some maniac." He took the letters from her, keeping his eyes on the window. "The parson seems to know all about him. Probably if we'd been getting the newspapers out here we'd know all about it too. Trouble is, we're so isolated."

"Isolated," she repeated, and took a small step toward the window. "There's no one else for miles."

"Of course there's this police cordon, and the parson chap." He, too, had lowered his voice.

"And why *us?*" she asked in a strained whisper, looking quickly at the letter in his hand.

"He's a maniac," Edward repeated. "He may be threatening lots of people." He gripped her suddenly by the shoulders. "Look, Joan darling. It's no use our standing here whispering and peering out of that damn window. Let's for God's sake get a grip on ourselves. Best thing we can do is get out of here."

"Out?" She was still peering at the emptiness of the moor in the late afternoon sunshine.

"It's less than six miles into Buckforth."

She said, as though she were talking to herself, "Over the moor."

"Only the first part. Chances are we'll run into one of the cops or the parson man on the way out, and this—what's-his-name?—Howard, he'll lie low till after dark, anyway."

"You think so?" She was still staring out of the window.

"Of course." His voice was loud and matter-of-fact. "His letter says tonight. I believe it's true that maniacs never shift from their plan. Kind of *idée fixe.* And anyway—in broad daylight. Now's when the going's good."

"All right." Her expression, as she turned quickly from the window, was a mixture of fear and unbelief in what was happening. "But if we're going, let's be quick. Let's go *now!*"

"Just a minute." He was looking about, with an air almost of embarrassment—as though he, too, hardly believed in the reality of danger—for some kind of weapon. He found a couple of sharp, sturdy kitchen knives and held one out to her awkwardly. "Only for just in case," he said. Her hand shook a little as she took it. She said, "I know. But it makes it all seem more horribly real."

He took a thick stick too, and she slung her handbag over her shoulder. As he pulled the door open, she managed a wavering smile. "And we were bored with our dull little cottage," she said.

"There might be tracks," he said from the threshold. "I suppose the parson came on his bicycle. Now I come to think of it, that must have been him we saw way off across the moor this morning."

"I couldn't see that far."

"I definitely saw someone off on the Buckforth road. Must have been him."

"If only we'd been here."

He was looking closely at the hard-earth path that led to the cottage door. "Too hard to hold tracks, I guess," he said. "Anyway, let's get going."

The moorland path went slantwise up and along the side of the steep ridge behind the cottage. They walked in the soft, bulging shadows of the tussocky heather, and their own shadows hurried beside them. Joan looked westward at the sun, going down toward a pile of thunderclouds.

"It's later than we thought," she said.

"We'll make it," he said. But he too looked westward, and now he was setting a pace that kept her nearly trotting behind him on the narrow track.

He could see her shadow out of the corner of his eye, and once he called out sharply, telling her not to keep looking back. "You can't get along that way," he said. "Besides, there's nothing there."

Before they quite reached the point where the path went over the saddle of the ridge, the thundercloud had hidden the sun. Their shadows had left them. On level ground at the top, they paused briefly, looking back and forward.

Ahead, the path dipped sharply down the long, steep eastern side of the ridge, into a glen at the bottom of which grass and bushes and tall trees took over from the heather. The light and color had drained away from the glen into a vague, early dusk. One could see the shape of the valley and where the trees and bushes were, but if one started to look hard at anything in particular, the details were softly blurred. The gurgle of the stream along the valley bottom, and the stirring of a small evening breeze in the heather and the treetops, blurred, too, the details of any other small sounds there might be.

They strained their eyes and ears against the gurgling, rustling dusk. "There could be anything down there," Joan said.

"Or nothing," Edward said sharply. "We'd better get on if we're going."

"Just let's listen for another second."

They stood rigid, listening. He said, "Come on," and stepped forward, and a paralyzing noise burst out of the valley and rushed up toward them. He jumped back as though something had hit him. For a split second the sound was everywhere. "It's the birds," Joan gasped. "They shot up all at once out of those trees down there."

They could see now the innumerable dark shapes of rooks circling and beginning to spiral down, with subsiding cries, toward the tops of the trees. "God, how they frightened me!" she said. "Just rooks."

But he was standing looking down intently. She looked at him and gripped his arm. "You mean something frightened *them,*" she whispered. He nodded, and as again they listened, both of them heard another sound, just audible through the scattered cawing of the rooks and the noise of the stream. Something was moving heavily in the undergrowth down there. Instinctively they both crouched in the heather. The noise stopped, then started again. It was impossible to tell whether it was a loud noise some way off, or a lesser noise in the nearest part of the valley bottom.

"Could be one of these moorland ponies," he whispered.

"We can't know."

The sound came again, the sound of a creature moving carefully.

"Too late," Joan breathed. "We can't go on." He nodded quickly. "The cottage is our best chance now."

Walking in a half crouch, they got back to the ridgetop. Then where the path dipped slantwise down the western flank, they started to run. The jolting thud of their feet and hearts deafened them to all other sounds. Panting painfully, they staggered together down the last narrow lap of the path to the cottage door. Then they stopped for the first time to look and listen.

Nothing could be seen or heard coming down the path. "We had a good start," Joan said.

Edward pushed her ahead of him into the house. "It may be only just enough," he said. "You get this door and window fixed. I'll do the front."

The cottage was a square box—two rooms in front, divided by a front door, which they never used, and a little passage running back to the kitchen, which filled the whole back space of the house. The front door was a heavy affair with bolts and chains that probably had not been opened in years. One of the little rooms they used only as a storeroom; the other was their bedroom. Edward moved quickly from one to the other, securing the heavy, old-fashioned shutters which had iron bars that locked them on the inside. When he returned, he found Joan had the kitchen windows shuttered, too, and the door barred. That was also a strong door, though the floor had sunk a couple of inches, leaving a gap through which the letters had been pushed sometime that morning.

A little of the dim remains of daylight still seeped in through large cracks in the shutters and between the heavy panels of the door. Edward lighted the oil lamp, set it on the floor, and rigged a curtain of dish towels around it so that it illuminated the room only dimly and wouldn't disclose them to a watcher outside.

"We'll want to keep a good ear open for the parson man," Edward said. "If he sees the place dark he may think we've gone."

They sat in the half-dark listening, and at the same moment both of them heard the noise of something coming down the path from the hillside. Edward had time to get up and tiptoe over to the door, hefting in his hand the small hatchet he had brought from the storeroom. Then a loud, authoritative hail came from outside. "Police out here. Anyone home?" Through the largest of the door's cracks, Edward caught a glimpse of the familiar uniform. He hurriedly unbarred and opened the door.

Edward interrupted the speech the policeman was beginning about having no wish to alarm them, but it was his duty to inform them that a maniac—

"We know a bit about that," Edward said. "Look at this." He handed the policeman the two letters.

"And what's more . . ." Joan began to tell the story of their attempted flight and the thing that had moved in the valley. The policeman listened stolidly. "Well, now," he said, "it might be as well to get that door shut, and if you'll get the lamp lit, I'll just take a look at all this."

Edward barred the door again. "That wouldn't have been anything but a moor pony," the policeman said. "Don't forget I've just come that way from Buckforth myself. Everything quiet. No birds whizzing about. For your information, the indications are that Howard's moving away from here. There'll be a police cordon between you and him by now," he said. "With dogs and all."

"But who *is* this Howard?" Joan asked.

"Barrington Howard?" he asked. "I thought everyone knew about that case."

Seven years ago, Howard, ex-acrobat, small-time actor, with nothing worse in the way of a police record than a couple of parking offenses, had murdered, with obscene brutality, five people in a single night. The victims were the members of two different families, living within a mile or so of one another in the outer suburbs. Both sets of victims were complete strangers to Howard. Each household had received, on the day before the murder, a notification of Howard's intention. "The same technique, you see," said the policeman, seeming to find satisfaction in the fact, as though it were a proof of order in a shifting world.

"But didn't the people he murdered—didn't they take precautions?" Joan asked.

"Seemingly didn't take enough," the policeman said grimly. In one case the recipients of the threat had dismissed it as an obvious practical joke by some friend of the family given to practical jokes. The other household had applied for, and received, a measure of police protection. Clearly it had not been sufficient because by some means which the killer would not, and his victims could not, disclose, Howard had gained admittance to both houses and carried out his threats to the letter. Obviously insane, he had been sent for life to the criminal lunatic asylum. Four days ago he had escaped.

"Queer thing how they caught him that first time," the policeman said. "It was psychological, kind of. He was very clever at disguising himself and he might have got clean away if it hadn't been for this psychology."

Psychiatry had broken through to Buckforth police station; the policeman knew the words. "Total recall" was the phrase he used to describe how Barrington Howard, despite his remarkably able disguise, had been picked up after those first and famous murders. Several people had known of him that he had what psychiatrists call "total recall" on one particular subject—Germany. It had been quite a joke in the suburban bar he used to frequent. If anyone brought up the subject of Germany, Howard had total recall —that is, he would get started talking about Germany, and go on recounting quite irrelevant and uninteresting facts about Germany, till, as the policeman said, the cows came home.

"Some people," the policeman explained, "just can remember everything about something—something they read, say, or something they saw. Where it's psychological is when they *have* to remember it. And they come out with it, too."

"Compulsive total recall," Edward said.

"The very words that were used," said the policeman approvingly. "That's the way they got him last time. Maybe that's how they'll get him this time. He's a plausible sort of chap, but they'll get him, all right. Don't you worry." He looked abruptly at his watch and fiddled with his hat.

Joan cried out, "But you're not going to leave us—like this— with that outside?"

The policeman shifted his weight from foot to foot.

"I know how you feel," he said, "but you see, the situation's like this . . ." The police already had had a message that the elderly farmer and his wife who lived in the most desolate part of the moor five miles to the westward had also received some kind of threat. The policeman's present assignment was to contact the officer in charge of the cordon, give him the message about the distant farm, and then go on ahead himself to guard duty there.

"Now," he said, "If I go against orders, the lieutenant won't get the message about the farm, and the old couple out there won't get any quick protection. No one but you and me knows about the letter you got. Seems to me, the only thing to do is for me to get going quickly, give them that information, and have them detail a man to come back here."

It made unanswerable good sense. Joan said, "You can't leave those two old people alone out there. With the killer near, perhaps." She gave a little shiver, and automatically her head turned toward the shuttered window.

"That's right." The policeman patted her arm. "Now look here,

I can tell you one thing: it's unlikely Howard's got hold of a gun, and even if he has, it's a hundred to one against his having more than a couple of rounds of ammo for it. And that means he can't shoot his way in here, and by the look of these shutters and the door, he'd have a hell of a time breaking his way in, either. Now, the parson that's written to you, he's a good chap—chaplain in a commando raid, he was—and before it's full dark *he'll* be here. With a gun, too, I expect. That should see you right till one of our men gets back here."

They listened to the policeman's bicycle bumping away, and then to the silence. Joan turned to her husband and looked into his eyes. "Anyway," she said, "We're together again." The wrangle of the morning seemed infinitely far away.

"Yes," he said, taking her in his arms, "We're together."

Suddenly she leaned away from him. "Listen," she said.

There was a sound on the path. Then there was a loud, repeated ringing of a bicycle bell, and a voice called out, "is that the Mansells? This is Beale. From Buckforth."

Edward called out in response. The voice came a little nearer, and then said, "Look, you'll probably want to take a look at me before you let me in. Do you want to open a shutter and shine a torch on me?"

"Okay." Edward opened the shutter a chink, and in the light of a flashlight surveyed the clerical figure standing rather stifly beside the bicycle a few yards away. He wore a conventional clerical collar, but otherwise he might have been, from his appearance, a doctor or government inspector, or some other kind of civil servant whose work was in the countryside. He grinned pleasantly at Edward. "No good taking chances," he said.

He was a biggish man, and when Edward, as he let him into the cottage and secured the door after him, commented that he looked like a useful reinforcement, he laughed and said that he had a bit more fighting experience than most chaplains.

They thanked him for his offer and prompt arrival.

"Well," he said, "if Howard is lurking round this bit of the moor the three of us ought to be a match for him. I brought a gun, just in case." He patted his pocket. "Now," he said, "what about showing me the defense plan?"

They showed him what they'd done, and he approved.

"There's nothing to do," he said, "but await developments.

Could you give me a sandwich, or something? I've been on the go all day and I'm pretty hungry."

Hurrying, Joan got the food. They carved cold ham and ate a lot of it, and had a potato salad. Edward brought out bottled beer from the cupboard and they drank that. They talked low and listened often. But with their new ally there, an armed ex-commando, there was a kind of gaiety in the tension now. It was like the first night of a war. And then, since the visitor seemed an exceptionally agreeable, as well as a kind and thoughtful man, Edward brought out, too, a bottle of whiskey which they had been saving.

As he did so, he saw Joan frown, and he said, "After all, if this isn't a special occasion, what is?" She smiled briefly. Their guest accepted a big shot of whiskey, and the men were soon deep in cheerful reminiscences about the war.

They kept refilling their glasses, even when Joan said, with a little extra emphasis, that she would not have any more because she thought everyone should have a clear head. She sat a little apart, frowning slightly in the gloom of the half-lighted kitchen. Edward accentuated his cheerfulness, as though to prove that he, at least, was a jolly good fellow who appreciated what another jolly good fellow was doing for them. And so he was still listening with a slightly fatuous smile for at least a quarter of a minute after Joan had stiffened suddenly in her chair.

"I entered Germany," the visitor was saying, "on the Cologne *Autobahn* at three forty-five on the morning of May the twentieth, 1945. I remember it as if it were yesterday. It made, this first sight of Germany, a quite unforgettable impression on me. Of course, when one comes to think of Germany, and the fate of Germany, and so on, naturally one . . ." His voice went on and on talking about Germany.

Edward's fatuous smile started to freeze on his face. Then, while the guest looked down into his glass, and talked about Germany, Edward got his smile back into position again and kept it there. At the first break in the stranger's talk, he started to rise and muttered something about going outside for a moment. Only outdoor sanitation here, you know, old boy."

The face above the clerical collar came up, alert and startled. "I really wouldn't do that, you know. I wouldn't take a chance on going out there alone. You don't realize how dangerous Howard is. I'll come along with you, though, if you like. I've got the gun, you see." His hand went to his pocket.

Edward relaxed into his chair, "Oh, well," he said, "later perhaps. We'll have another drink first, anyway." The other relaxed, too. "I'm not going to let you out of my sight," he said, smiling.

Keeping it slow and casual, Edward leaned forward to take the bottle. "I'll fill that up for you," he said. The other looked at his glass, and as he did so, Edward got the neck of the bottle in his fist, jumped suddenly from his chair, and swung with what force he could at the side of the lowered head in front of him. The other rolled sideways and seemed to be trying to get out of his chair. His mouth came open, and his eyes stared up with the look of a man taken utterly by surprise. Before he could even make a move to handle his gun, Edward hit him again. With a deep, shuddering groan, the man toppled right out of the chair.

For a couple of seconds, Edward stood, staring down at him, incredulous at the success of his act. Then he began to claw at his own necktie, ripped it off, and started awkwardly binding the man's hands behind him. Joan dashed to the cupboard and came back again with a length of clothesline. Silently, trembling with delayed terror, they trussed the big man's arms and legs, twisting the rope around him in a frenzy of self-protection.

The bound man was breathing heavily. Edward felt the side of his head with his fingertips and decided there was no fracture. They tied a wet dishcloth over the small bleeding wound the bottle had made. They stood back, looking first at the helpless figure on the floor, then at each other. Relief flooded through them. For a minute or two they babbled at each other. "It was my fault," Edward heard himself saying. "I took a couple too many drinks. He fooled me completely."

"But, darling," Joan was saying, "He'd have taken in anybody."

Edward looked at her gratefully, and then out of the corner of his eye he saw a movement on the floor. The man's leg had moved, gently, stealthily, and one of the knots they had tied loosened and slipped.

Edward's voice came in a sharp whisper. "Look out," he said. "He's moving. He's—you remember what the policeman said— he's an acrobat. He may be a kind of Houdini."

Fear came back into the room. The prisoner was motionless now, his eyes still closed, but his immobility had the suggestion of a sinister trick. They stared down at him and actually wished that he would make another movement, something that would give an indication of what he planned. But he did nothing. And they, watching him in fascination, began to have the sensation that quite suddenly, in a single second perhaps, he would simply leap out of the knots and the clothesline and go for them.

"My God," said Joan. "I can't stand this all night."

There was no telephone at the cottage, and Edward said, "I'm afraid all night is what it's going to be. We could take turns watching."

"I wouldn't dare be alone with—that."

"We could drag him into the front room and lock him in."

They were talking in whispers now.

"It might be just his chance," Joan said. "While we were lifting him, he might get loose. They can get out of anything, people trained to do those tricks."

It was as though the man on the floor had established some commanding position, as though they, and not he, were helpless.

"Maybe," said Joan suddenly, "the real Mr. Beale, the real parson will turn up."

Edward looked at his watch and saw to his surprise that even after all that had happened it was still early. Mr. Beale probably would keep his word and "look in" on his way back from what he had called the "outer edge" of the parish.

"I hope to God he comes," Edward said.

For a half hour that seemed a lot longer, they sat, not daring to take their eyes off the figure on the floor. Once Edward thought he saw a new, stealthy movement of an arm, and went over and tried to tighten one of their knots, which now looked horribly amateurish. And then they heard the repeated ringing of a bicycle bell out in the dark, and a voice hailing them.

"It's me, Beale," shouted the voice. "Are you all right?" His voice had a note of urgent anxiety.

"Yes. We're all right." Edward's voice was a little shaky. With an effort, as though he might be struck suddenly in the back, he went across to the door and started to unbolt it.

The man outside said, "I really ought to give you some kind of password."

But Edward already had the door open and was explaining the situation.

The other stepped quickly across the room to look at the man on the floor.

"My goodness," he said, "he really does look like a parson, doesn't he? Though," he added, "if you were entirely familiar with the behavior of parsons these days, you might have thought his getup a little, well, a little *too* parsonical."

He himself wore a clerical collar, but was otherwise dressed in rather crumpled light-gray flannels.

He bent over the bound man, and fingered the knots.

"If you'd just give me a hand," he said, "I think we could tighten up this job here and there. And what about the gun? Didn't you say he had a gun?"

Edward gasped. He realized that in the excitement of knocking the man out and then tying him up, he had forgotten the gun.

The newcomer fumbled for it with slightly shaking hands and finally pulled it out of the man's side pocket. "Well," he said, "he seems safe enough now. There's not much trouble he can cause now."

Belatedly they offered him a drink.

"The thing I don't understand," Joan said, "is how this maniac *knew* that you were going to come here. I can understand his picking on us as his victims because of it being so lonely here. But how did he know he could get in right away by pretending to be you?"

"You see your note," said Edward, "was pushed in after his. It was nearer the door and must have pushed his along the floor."

The other looked at him with raised eyebrows.

"But I didn't push mine under the door at all," he said. "I pinned it to the door. Stupid thing to do, now I come to think of it. In fact, if I weren't a parson, I'd call it a *damn* stupid thing to do. Howard must have found it, read it, resealed it, and pushed it under the door. That's how he was able to make his plan. Didn't you notice anything funny about the envelope?"

They remembered their bitter quarreling in the afternoon. They had not been in a noticing mood. "We didn't notice anything," Joan said sadly.

"And when *did* you notice anything?"

"When he had that 'total recall' thing about Germany," Joan said. "The policeman had told us about his peculiarity. Edward said something about Germany, and suddenly there he was having 'total recall.' "

"Talked about Germany, did he?" said the other interestedly. "Now I could tell you quite a lot about Germany. I will commence with essential statistics of the area of the country, principal exports and imports, industrial and agricultural production, outstanding historical events. Taking the production figures for 1939, and comparing them with those for 1948, 1949 and the first quarter of 1950, we get a statistical picture of Germany susceptible of comparison with the statistical picture of pre-Hitler Germany."

Edward saw the man pick up the knife while he talked, and at the same time he heard Joan's dreadful scream.

A good bit of crime fiction has explored the subject of the perfect crime—or, to be more precise, the crime which would have been perfect except for one little detail. The truly perfect crimes, in real life, are the ones we never hear about, and in fiction, unless handled very well indeed, they tend to upset our sense of justice, or our anticipations. But let's take the perfect crime one step further —to its victim. What recourse has he? None in law, of course, by definition. But isn't there a chance that somehow, sometimes, the scales might be balanced, as in this ingenious tale from the 1953 anthology?

HARRY MUHEIM

The Dusty Drawer

Norman Logan paid for his apple pie and coffee, then carried his tray toward the front of the cafeteria. From a distance, he recognized the back of William Tritt's large head. The tables near Tritt were empty, and Logan had no desire to eat with him, but they had some unfinished business that Logan wanted to clear up. He stopped at Tritt's table and asked, "Do you mind if I join you?"

Tritt looked up as he always looked up from inside his teller's cage in the bank across the street. He acted like a servant—like a fat, precise butler that Logan used to see in movies—but behind the film of obsequiousness was an attitude of vast superiority that always set Logan on edge.

"Why, yes, Mr. Logan. Do sit down. Only please, I must ask you not to mention that two hundred dollars again."

"Well, we'll see about that," said Logan, pulling out a chair and seating himself. "Rather late for lunch, isn't it?"

"Oh, I've had lunch," Tritt said. "This is just a snack." He cut a large piece of roast beef from the slab in front of him and thrust it into his mouth. "I don't believe I've seen you all summer," he added, chewing the meat.

"I took a job upstate," Logan said. "We were trying to stop some kind of blight in the apple orchards."

"Is that so?" Tritt looked like a concerned bloodhound.

"I wanted to do some research out West," Logan went on, "but I couldn't get any money from the university."

"You'll be back for the new term, won't you?"

"Oh, yes," Logan said with a sigh, "we begin again tomorrow." He thought for a moment of the freshman faces that would be looking up at him in the lecture room. A bunch of high-strung, mechanical New York City kids, pushed by their parents or by the Army into the university, and pushed by the university into his botany class. They were brick-bound people who had no interest in growing things, and Logan sometimes felt sad that in five years of teaching he had communicated to only a few of them his own delight with his subject.

"My, one certainly gets a long vacation in the teaching profession," Tritt said. "June through September."

"I suppose," Logan said. "Only trouble is that you don't make enough to do anything in all that spare time."

Tritt laughed a little, controlled laugh and continued chewing. Logan began to eat the pie. It had the drab, neutral flavor of all cafeteria pies.

"Mr. Tritt," he said, after a long silence.

"Yes?"

"When are you going to give me back my two hundred dollars?"

"Oh, come now, Mr. Logan. We had this all out ten months ago. We went over it with Mr. Pinkson and the bank examiners and everyone. I did *not* steal two hundred dollars from you."

"You did, and you know it."

"Frankly, I'd rather not hear any more about it."

"Mr. Tritt, I had three hundred and twenty-four dollars in my hand that day. I'd just cashed some bonds. I know how much I had."

"The matter has all been cleared up," Tritt said coldly.

"Not for me, it hasn't. When you entered the amount in my checking account, it was for one hundred and twenty-four, not three hundred twenty-four."

Tritt put down his fork and carefully folded his hands. "I've heard you tell that story a thousand times, sir. My cash balanced when you came back and complained."

"Sure it balanced," Logan exploded. "You saw your mistake when Pinkson asked you to check the cash. So you took my two hundred out of the drawer. No wonder it balanced!"

Tritt laid a restraining hand on Logan's arm. "Mr. Logan, I'm going a long, long way in the bank. I simply can't afford to make mistakes."

"You also can't afford to admit it when you do make one."

"Oh, come now," said Tritt, as though he were speaking to a child. "Do you think I'd jeopardize my entire career for two hundred dollars?"

"You didn't jeopardize your career," Logan snapped. "You knew you could get away with it. And you took my money to cover your error."

Tritt sat calmly and smiled a fat smile at Logan. "Well, that's your version, Mr. Logan. But I do wish you'd quit annoying me with your fairy tale." Leaving half his meat untouched, Tritt stood up and put on his hat. Then he came around the table and stood looming over Logan. "I will say, however, from a purely hypothetical point of view, that if I *had* stolen your money and then staked my reputation on the lie that I hadn't, the worst thing I could possibly do would be to return the money to you. I think you'd agree with that."

"I'll get you, Tritt," said Logan, sitting back in the chair. "I can't stand to be had."

"I know, I know. You've been saying that for ten months, too. Good-by, now."

Tritt walked out of the cafeteria. Norman Logan sat there motionless, watching the big teller cross the street and enter the bank. He felt no rage—only an increased sense of futility. Slowly, he finished his coffee.

A few minutes later, Logan entered the bank. Down in the safe-deposit vaults, he raised the lid of his long metal box an took out three twenty-five dollar bonds. With a sigh, he began to fill them out for cashing. They would cover his government insurance premium for the year. In July, too, he'd taken three bonds from the box, when his father had over-spent his pension money. And earlier in the summer, Logan had cashed some more of them, after slamming into a truck and damaging his Plymouth. Almost every month there was some reason to cash bonds, and Logan reflected that he hadn't bought one since his Navy days. There just wasn't enough money in botany.

With the bonds in his hand, he climbed the narrow flight of stairs to the street floor, then walked past the long row of tellers' cages to the rear of the bank. Here he opened an iron gate in a low marble fence and entered the green-carpeted area of the manager and assistant manager. The manager's desk was right inside the gate, and Mr. Pinkson looked up as Logan came in. He smiled, looking over the top of the glasses pinched on his nose.

"Good afternoon, Mr. Logan." Pinkson's quick eyes went to the bonds and then, with the professional neutrality of a branch bank manager, right back up to Logan's thin face. "If you'll just sit down, I'll buzz Mr. Tritt."

"Mr. Tritt?" said Logan, surprised.

"Yes. He's been moved up to the first cage now."

Pinkson indicated a large, heavy table set far over against the side wall in back of his desk, and Logan sat in a chair next to it.

"Have a good summer?" The little man had revolved in his squeaky executive's chair to face Logan.

"Not bad, thanks."

"Did you get out of the city?"

"Yes, I had a job upstate. I always work during my vacations."

Mr. Pinkson let out a controlled chuckle, a suitable reply when he wasn't sure whether or not the customer was trying to be funny. Then he revolved again; his chubby cue-ball head bobbed down, and he was back at his figures.

Logan put the bonds on the clean desk blotter and looked over at Tritt's cage. It was at the end of the row of cages, with a door opening directly into the manager's area. Tritt was talking on the telephone inside, and for a long, unpleasant minute Logan watched the fat, self-assured face through the greenish glass. I'll get him yet, Logan thought. But he didn't see how. Tritt had been standing firmly shielded behind his lie for nearly a year now, and Norman Logan didn't seem to know enough about vengeance to get him.

Restive, Logan sat back and tipped the chair onto its hind legs. He picked ineffectually at a gravy stain on his coat; then his eye was attracted to a drawer, hidden under the overhang of the table-top. It was a difficult thing to see, for it had no handle, and its face was outlined by only a thin black crack in the dark-stained wood. Logan could see faintly the two putty-filled holes that marked the place where the handle had once been. Curious, he rocked forward a little and slipped his fingernails into the crack along the bottom of the drawer. He pulled gently, and the drawer slid smoothly and silently from the table.

The inside was a dirty, cluttered mess. Little mounds of grayish mold had formed on the furniture glue along the joints. A film of dust on the bottom covered the bits of faded yellow paper and rusted paper clips that were scattered about. Logan rocked the chair back farther, and the drawer came far out to reveal a delicate spider web. The spider was dead and flaky, resting on an old page from a desk calendar. The single calendar sheet read October 2, 1936. Logan pushed the drawer softly back into the table, wondering if it had actually remained closed since Alf Landon was running against Roosevelt.

The door of Tritt's cage clicked open, and he came out, carrying a large yellow form. William Tritt moved smoothly across the carpet, holding his fat young body erect and making a clear effort to keep his stomach in.

"Why hello, Mr. Logan," he said. "I'm sorry for the delay. The main office called me. I can't hang up on them, you know."

"I know," Logan said.

The teller smiled as he lowered himself into the chair opposite Logan. Logan slid the bonds across the table.

"It's nice to see you again," Tritt said pleasantly as he opened his fountain pen. "Preparing for the new semester, I suppose?" There was no indication of their meeting across the street. Logan said nothing in reply, so Tritt went to work, referring rapidly to the form for the amount to be paid on each bond. "Well, that comes to sixty-seven dollars and twenty-five cents," he said, finishing the addition quickly.

Logan filled out a deposit slip. "Will you put it in my checking account, please?" He handed his passbook across the table. "And will you please enter the right amount?"

"Certainly, Mr. Logan," Tritt said, smiling indulgently. Logan watched carefully as Tritt made the entry. Then the teller walked rapidly back to his cage, while Logan, feeling somehow compelled to do so, took another glance into the dusty drawer. He kept thinking about the drawer as he got on a bus and rode up to the university. It had surprised him to stumble upon a dirty, forgotten place like that in a bank that was always so tidy.

Back in the biology department, Logan sat down at his desk, planning to prepare some roll sheets for his new classes. He stayed there for a long time without moving. The September sun went low behind the New Jersey Palisades, but he did not prepare the sheets, for the unused drawer stayed unaccountably in his mind.

Suddenly he sat forward in his chair. In a surprising flash of creative thought, he had seen how he could make use of the drawer. He wasn't conscious of having tried to develop a plan. The entire plan simply burst upon him all at once, and with such clarity and precision that he hardly felt any responsibility for it. He would rob the bank and pin the robbery on Tritt. That would take care of Tritt . . .

In the weeks that followed, Norman Logan remained surprisingly calm about his plan. Each time he went step by step over the mechanics of the robbery, it seemed more gemlike and more workable. He made his first move the day he got his November pay check.

Down on Fifty-first Street, Logan went into a novelty-and-trick store and bought a cigarette case. It was made of a dark, steel-blue plastic, and it looked like a trim thirty-eight automatic. When the trigger was pressed, a section of the top of the gun flipped upon a hinge, revealing the cigarettes inside the handle.

With this in his pocket, Logan took a bus way down to the lower part of Second Avenue and entered a grimy little shop displaying pistols and rifles in the window. The small shopkeeper shuffled forward, and Logan asked to see a thirty-eight.

"Can't sell you a thing until I see your permit," the man said. "The Sullivan Law."

"Oh, I don't want to buy a weapon," Logan explained. He took out his plastic gun. "I just want to see if the real thing looks like mine here."

The little man laughed a cackle laugh and brought up a thirty-eight from beneath the counter, placing it next to Logan's. "So you'll just be fooling around, eh?"

"That's right," said Logan, looking at the guns. They were almost identical.

"Oh, they look enough alike," said the man. "But lemme give you a little tip. Put some Scotch tape over that lid to keep it down. Friend of mine was using one of those things, mister. He'd just polished off a stick-up when he pulled the trigger and the lid flopped open. Well, he tried to offer the victim a cigarette, but the victim hauled off and beat the hell out of him."

"Thanks," Logan said with a smile. "I'll remember that."

"Here, you can put some Scotch tape on right now."

Logan walked over to the Lexington Avenue line and rode uptown on the subway. It was five minutes to three when he got to the bank. The old, gray-uniformed guard touched his cap as Logan came through the door. The stand-up desks were crowded, so it was natural enough for Logan to go through the little iron gate and across to the table with the drawer. Mr. Pinkson and the new assistant manager had already left; their desks were clear. As Logan sat down, Tritt stuck his head out the door of his cage.

"More bonds, Mr. Logan?" he asked.

"No," said Logan. "Just a deposit."

Tritt closed the door and bent over his work. Logan took out his wallet, removed the pay check, then looked carefully the length of the bank. No one was looking in his direction. As he put the wallet back into his inside coat pocket, he withdrew the slim plastic gun and eased open the drawer. He dropped the gun in, shut the drawer, deposited the check, and went home to his apartment In spite of the Sullivan Law, he was on his way.

Twice during November he used the table with the drawer Each time he checked on the gun. It had not been moved. By the time he deposited his December check, Logan was completely certain that nobody ever looked in there. On the nineteenth of th month, he decided to take the big step.

Next morning, after his ten-o'clock class, Logan walked si blocks through the snow down the hill to the bank. He took fou bonds out of his safe-deposit box and filled them out for cashing. The soothing sound of recorded Christmas carols floated down from the main floor.

Upstairs, he seated himself at the heavy table to wait for Tritt. Pinkson had nodded and returned to his figuring; the nervous assistant manager was not around. The carols were quite loud here, and Logan smiled at this unexpected advantage. He placed the bonds squarely on the blotter. Then he slipped open the drawer, took out the gun with his left hand, and held it below the table.

Tritt was coming toward him, carrying his bond chart. They said hello, and Tritt sat down and went to work. He totaled the sum twice and said carefully, still looking at the figures, "Well, Mr. Logan, that comes to eighty-three fifty."

"I'll want something in addition to the eighty-three fifty," said Logan, leaning forward and speaking in an even voice.

"What's that?" asked Tritt.

"Ten thousand dollars in twenty-dollar bills."

Tritt's pink face smiled. He started to look up into Logan's face, but his eyes froze on the muzzle of the gun poking over the edge of the table. He did not notice that Scotch tape.

"Now just go to your cage and get the money," Logan said. It was William Tritt's first experience with anything like this. "Mr. Logan. Come now, Mr. Logan . . ." He swallowed and tried to start again, but his self-assurance had deserted him. He turned toward Pinkson's back.

"Look at me," snapped Logan.

Tritt turned back. "Mr. Logan, you don't know what you're doing."

"Keep still."

"Couldn't we give you a loan or perhaps a—"

"Listen to me, Tritt." Logan's voice was just strong enough to carry above The First Noel. He was amazed at how authoritative he sounded. "Bring the money in a bag. Place it on the table here."

Tritt started to object, but Logan raised the gun slightly, and the last resistance drained from Tritt's fat body.

"All right, all right. I'll get it." As Tritt moved erratically toward his cage, Logan dropped the gun back into the drawer and closed it. Tritt shut the door of the cage, and his head disappeared below the frosted part of the glass. Immediately, Mr. Pinkson's telephone buzzed, and he picked it up. Logan watched his back, and after a few seconds, Pinkson's body stiffened. Logan sighed, knowing then that he would not get the money on this try.

Nothing happened for several seconds; then suddenly the little old guard came rushing around the corner of the cages, his big pistol drawn and wobbling as he tried to hold it on Logan.

"Okay. Okay. Stay there! Put your hands up, now!"

Logan raised his hands, and the guard turned to Pinkson with a half-surprised face. "Okay, Mr. Pinkson. Okay, I've got him covered now."

Pinkson got up as Tritt came out of the cage. Behind the one gun, the three men came slowly toward Logan.

"Careful, Louie, he's armed," Tritt warned the guard.

"May I ask what this is all about?" Logan said, his hands held high.

"Mr. Logan," said Pinkson, "I'm sorry about this, but Mr. Tritt here tells me that—that—"

"That you tried to rob me of ten thousand dollars," said Tritt, his voice choppy.

"I—I *what?*"

"You just attempted an armed robbery of this bank," Tritt said slowly. "Don't try to deny it."

Logan's face became the face of a man so completely incredulous that he cannot speak. He remembered not to overplay it, though. First he simply laughed at Tritt. Then he lowered his hands, regardless of the guard's gun, and stood up, the calm, indignant faculty member.

"All I can say, Mr. Tritt, is that I do deny it."

"Goodness," said Pinkson.

"Better take his gun, Louie," Tritt ordered the guard.

The guard stepped gingerly forward to Logan and frisked him, movie style. "Hasn't got a gun, Mr. Tritt," he said.

"Of course he's got a gun," snapped Tritt. He pushed the guard aside. "It's right in his coat." Tritt jammed his thick hand into Logan's left coat pocket and flailed it about. "It's not in that pocket," he said after a moment.

"It's not in any pocket," Logan said. "I don't have one."

"You do. You *do* have a gun. I saw it," Tritt answered, beginning to sound like a child in an argument. He spun Logan around and pulled the coat off him with a jerk. The sleeves turned inside out. Eagerly, the teller pulled the side pockets out, checked the inside pocket and the breast pocket, then ran his hands over the entire garment, crumpling it. "The—the gun's not in his coat," he said finally.

"It's not in his pants," the guard added.

Tritt stepped over to the table quickly. "It's around here somewhere," he said. "We were sitting right here." He stood directly in front of the closed drawer, and his hands began to move meaninglessly over the tabletop. He picked up the neat stack of deposit slips, put them down again, then looked under the desk blotter, as though it could have concealed a gun.

Logan knew he had to stop this. "Is there any place I can remove the rest of my clothes?" he asked loudly, slipping the suspenders from his shoulders. Several depositors had gathered on the other side of the marble fence to watch, and Mr. Pinkson had had enough.

"Oh, no, no," he said, almost shouting. "That won't be necessary, Mr. Logan. Louie said you were unarmed. Now, Louie, put *your* gun away, and for goodness' sake, request the customers to please move on."

"But Mr. Pinkson, you must believe me," Tritt said, coming over to the manager. "This man held a gun on me and—"

"It's hard to know what to believe," said Pinkson. "But no money was stolen, and I don't see how we can embarrass Mr. Logan further with this matter. Please, Mr. Logan, do pull up your suspenders."

It was a shattering moment for the teller—the first time his word had ever been doubted at the bank.

"But sir, I insist that this man—"

"I must ask you to return to your cage now, Mr. Tritt," Pinkson said, badly agitated. Tritt obeyed.

The manager helped Logan put on his coat, then steered him over to his desk. "This is all a terrible mistake, Mr. Logan. Please do sit down now, please." The friendly little man was breathing heavily. "Now, I just want you to know that if you should press this complaint, it—it would go awfully bad for us down in the main office downtown, and I—"

"Please don't get excited, Mr. Pinkson," Logan said with a smile. "I'm not going to make any complaint." Logan passed the whole thing off casually. Mr. Tritt imagined he saw a gun, that's all. It was simply one of those aberrations that perfectly normal people get occasionally. Now, could Mr. Pinkson finish cashing his bonds? The manager paid him the eighty-three fifty, continuing to apologize.

Logan left the bank and walked through the soft snowfall, whistling a Christmas carol. He'd handled himself perfectly.

In the weeks that followed, Logan continued to do business with Tritt, just as though nothing had happened. The teller tried to remain aloof and calm, but he added sums incorrectly, and his hands shook. One day late in January, Tritt stood up halfway through a transaction, his great body trembling, "Excuse me, Mr. Logan," he murmured, and rushed off into the corridor behind the cages. Pinkson followed him, and Logan took advantage of the moment to check on the gun. It lay untouched in the drawer. Then Pinkson came back alone. "I'm awfully sorry to delay you again, sir," he said. "Mr. Tritt doesn't feel too well."

"Did he imagine he saw another gun?" Logan asked quietly.

"No. He just upsets easily now. Ever since that incident with you last month, he's been like a cat on a hot stove."

"I've noticed he's changed."

"He's lost that old, calm banking touch, Mr. Logan. And of course, he's in constant fear of a new hallucination."

"I'm sorry to hear that," Logan said, looking genuinely concerned. "It's very sad when a person loses his grip."

"It's particularly disappointing to me," the manager said sadly. "I brought Tritt into the bank myself, you see. Had him earmarked for a big spot downtown someday. Fine man. Intelligent, steady, accurate—why, he's been right down the line on everything. But now—now he's—well, I *do* hope he gets over this."

"I can understand how you feel," Logan said sympathetically He smiled inside at the precision of his planning. Fat William Tritt had been undermined just enough—not only in Pinkson' mind, but in his own.

On the tenth of March, Norman Logan acted again. When Trit was seated across the table from him, Logan said, "Well, here w go again, Mr. Tritt." Tritt's head came up, and once more he wa looking into the barrel of the toy automatic. He did not try t speak. "Now go get the ten thousand," ordered Logan. "And th time, do it."

Without objecting, the teller moved quickly to his cage. Logan slipped the gun back into the drawer; then he took his brief case from the door and stood it on the edge of the table. Pinkson's telephone didn't buzz, and the guard remained out of sight. After a few moments, Tritt came out of the cage, carrying a small cloth bag.

"All right, continue with the bonds," Logan said. "The bag goes on the table between us." Logan shifted forward and opened the bag, keeping the money out of sight behind the brief case. The clean new bills were wrapped in thousand-dollar units, each package bound with a bright yellow strip of paper. Logan counted through one package, and, with Tritt looking right at him, he placed the package of money carefully in the brief case.

"There," he said. "Now finish with the bonds." Tritt finished filling out the form and got Logan's signature. He was not as flustered as Logan had thought he'd be. "Now listen, Tritt," Logan went on, "my getaway is all set, of course, but if you give any signal before I'm out of the bank, I'll put a bullet into you—right here." Logan pointed to the bridge of his own nose. "Please don't think I'd hesitate to do it. Now get back to your cage."

Tritt returned to the cage. While his back was turned, Logan slipped the bag of money from his brief case and dropped it into the drawer, next to the gun. He eased the drawer into the table, took the brief case, and walked out of the bank.

Outside, he stood directly in front of the entrance, as though he were waiting for a bus. After just a few seconds, the burglar alarm went off with a tremendous electrical shriek, and the old guard came running out of the door after him.

He was followed immediately by Pinkson, the assistant manager, and Tritt.

"Well, gentlemen," said Logan, his hands raised again in front of the guard's gun, "here we are again, eh?"

A crowd was gathering, and Pinkson sent the assistant to turn off the alarm. "Come, let's all go inside," he said. "I don't want any fuss out here."

It was the same kind of scene that they'd played before, only now Logan—the twice-wronged citizen—was irate, and now ten thousand dollars was missing from William Tritt's cage. Tritt was calm, though.

"I was ready for him this time," he said proudly to Pinkson. "I marked ten thousand worth of twenties. My initial is on the band. The money's in his brief case."

"Oh, for Heaven's sake, Tritt," Logan shouted suddenly, "who ever heard of making a getaway by waiting for a bus. I don't know what your game is, but—"

"Never mind my game," said Tritt. "Let's just take a look in your brief case."

He wrenched it from Logan's hand, clicked the lock, and turned the brief case upside down. A group of corrected examination books fell out. That was all.

"See?" said Logan. "Not a cent." The guard put away his gun as Pinkson began to pick up the scattered books.

Tritt wheeled, threw the brief case against the wall, and grabbed Logan by the lapels. "But I gave you the money. I did. I did!" His face was a pasty gray, and his voice high. "You put it in the brief case. I saw you. I *saw* you do it!" He began to shake Logan in a kind of final attempt to shake the ten thousand dollars out of him.

Pinkson straightened up with the exam books and said, "For goodness' sake, Mr. Tritt. Stop it. Stop it."

Tritt stopped shaking Logan, then turned wildly to Pinkson. "You don't believe me!" he shouted. "You don't believe me!" he shouted. "You don't believe me!"

"It's not a question of—"

"I'll find that money. I'll show you who's lying." He rushed over to the big table and swept it completely clear with one wave of his heavy arm. The slips fluttered to the floor, and the inkwell broke, splattering black ink over the carpet. Tritt pulled the table in a wild, crashing arc across the green carpet, smashing it into Pinkson's desk. Logan saw the dusty drawer come open about a half-inch.

The big man dropped clumsily to his knees and began to pound on the carpet with his flattened hands as he kept muttering, "It' around here someplace—a cloth bag." He grabbed a corner of the carpet and flipped it back with a grunt. It made a puff of dust and revealed only a large triangle of empty, dirty floor. A dozen people had gathered outside the marble fence by now, and all the tellers were peering through the glass panes of the cages at Tritt.

"I'll find it! I'll find it!" he shouted. A film of sweat was on h forehead as he stood up, turned, and advanced again toward the table. The slightly opened drawer was in plain sight in front of him, but everyone's eyes were fixed on Tritt, and Tritt did not see the drawer under the overhang of the table.

Logan turned quickly to Pinkson and whispered, "He may be dangerous, Mr. Pinkson. You've got to calm him." He grabbed Pinkson by the arm and pushed him backward several feet, so that the manager came to rest on the edge of the table, directly over the drawer. The exam books were still in his hand.

"Mr. Tritt, you *must* stop this!" Mr. Pinkson said.

"Get out of my way, Pinkson," said Tritt, coming right at him, breathing like a bull. "You believe him, but I'll show you. I'll find it!" He placed his hands on Pinkson's shoulders. "Now get away, you fool."

"I won't take that from anyone," snapped Pinkson. He slapped Tritt's face with a loud, stinging blow. The teller stopped, stunned, and suddenly began to cry.

"Mr. Pinkson. Mr. Pinkson, you've *got* to trust me."

Pinkson was immediately ashamed of what he had done. "I'm sorry, my boy. I shouldn't have done that."

"I tell you he held a gun on me again. A real gun—it's not my imagination."

"But why didn't you call Louie?" Pinkson said. "That's the rule, you know."

"I wanted to catch him myself. He—he made such a fool of me last month."

"But that business last month was hallucination," said Pinkson, looking over at Logan. Logan nodded.

"It's no hallucination when ten thousand dollars is missing," Tritt shouted.

"That's precisely where the confusion arises in my mind," Mr. Pinkson said slowly. "We'll get it straight, but in the meantime, I must order your arrest, Mr. Tritt."

Logan came and stood next to Pinkson, and they both looked sympathetically at the teller as he walked slowly, still sobbing, back to the cage.

"I'm just sick about it," Pinkson said.

"I think you'll find he's not legally competent," said Logan, putting a comforting thought into Pinkson's head.

"Perhaps not."

Logan showed his concern by helping to clean up the mess that Tritt had made. He and the assistant manager placed the table back into its position against the far wall, Logan shoving the dusty drawer firmly closed with his fingertips as they lifted it.

Norman Logan returned to the bank late the next day. He sat at the table to make a deposit, and he felt a pleasantly victorious sensation surge through him as he slipped the gun and the ten thousand dollars out of the drawer and into his overcoat pocket. As he walked out the front door past the guard, he met Mr. Pinkson, who was rushing in.

"Terrible, Terrible," the little man said, without even pausing to say hello.

"What's that?" Logan asked calmly.

"I've just been talking to the doctors at Bellevue about Tritt," Pinkson said. "He seems all right, and they've released him. Unfortunately, he can answer every question except 'Where's the money?' " Logan held firmly to the money in his pocket and continued to extend his sympathies.

Back at his apartment, Logan borrowed a portable typewriter from the man upstairs. Then he sat down and wrote a note:

Dear Mr. Pinkson:
  I'm returning the money. I'm so sorry. I guess I didn't know what I was doing. I guess I haven't known for some time.

After looking up Tritt's initials on an old deposit slip, he forged a small tidy *W.T.* to the note.

Logan wiped his fingerprints from the bills and wrapped them, along with the note, in a neat package. For one delicious moment he considered how nice it would be to hang on to the money. He could resign from the university, go out West, and continue his research on his own. But that wasn't part of the plan, and the plan was working too well to tamper with it now. Logan drove to the post office nearest Tritt's apartment and mailed the money to Pinkson at the bank.

In the morning, Mr. Pinkson telephoned Logan at the university. "Well, it's all cleared up," he said, relieved but sad. "Tritt returned the money, so the bank is not going to press the charges. Needless to say, we're dropping Tritt. He not only denies having taken the money, he also denies having returned it."

"I guess he just doesn't know what he's doing," Logan said.

"Yes. That's what he said in the note. Anyway, Mr. Logan, I —I just wanted to call and apologize for the trouble we've caused you."

"Oh, it was no trouble for me," Logan replied, smiling.

"And you've been very helpful, too," Pinkson added.

"I was glad to be of help," Logan said quietly. "Delighted, in fact."

They said good-by then, and Logan walked across the hall to begin his ten-o'clock botany lecture.

The straightforward murder, committed for gain or revenge or some other comprehensible motive, may have its own kind of horror; but what of those bestialities—inexplicable and unforesee-able—that may rise from the murky depths of the human mind, as in . . .

MORTON WOLSON

The Attacker

Caught in the focus of spotlights from three patrol cars, the blonde stood defiant, resisting an intern, Sergeant Murphy, and hysteria. In that order.

This was evident as Patrolman Jaffe braked my sedan on the footpath alongside the ambulance. The blonde screamed alter-nately at the intern and Murphy, who respectively wheeled and shouted back at her.

No onlookers. At 3 in the morning, following a slight shower, deep in Riverside Park, any onlooker would have been booked on suspicion automatically.

My stomach tightened as Plainclothesman Carson drifted to my window. "I found her unconscious, Captain."

"Where?"

He pointed to a KEEP OFF THE GRASS sign. "Alongside that. She came to just before the ambulance got here. Her story's different. So's she."

"Why doesn't she get in the ambulance?"

"Afraid of publicity. She wants us to forget it. Don't want med-ical attention, to make a complaint, or anything. Just we should take her to a friend's house where she'll wash and borrow a dress and then tell hubby she got lost in the subway or somethin'."

Mud smeared her from platinum coiffure to eggshell blue pumps. Her dress had been eggshell blue. No way to tell, through the grime, whether she was pretty. Probably she was. The others had been.

I listened to Sergeant Murphy damn her husband and then say: "The *guy,* honey—concentrate on the *guy!* All the time you're stallin' he's runnin'!"

"I didn't *see* him!" she screamed back. "Can't you get that through your thick head?"

Murphy switched to patient logic—at the top of his lungs. "This guy calls you to his car parked on upper Broadway. He asks you how to reach the Bronx. You step over to tell him. He shows you a gun. When you're in, he clobbers you unconscious. You mean to say you can't tell us he's tall, short, fat, thin, young, old, light, dark—*anything?*"

She fainted.

The intern and a patrolman caught her. They got her into the ambulance. It drove off.

Murphy launched all hands on a flashlight search of the area. I asked Carson, "What's different about her, aside from her story?"

His small eyes glistened. He was a large, redheaded man with a good record on the force. I disliked him.

"You seen her," his tone snickered. "You ever see a dame stacked like that off a burlesque runway, Cap'n?"

Instead of replying I grabbed my flashlight, stepped to the grass, and motioned him to follow.

The pattern was all wrong. She couldn't have picked up mud smears near that KEEP OFF THE GRASS sign. And he didn't take his victims to parks. He found them there. In company.

We descended the damp, grassy slope until my flash beam found a wide patch of drying mud. Across one side of it was a series of impressions that could have been made by high heels. Following an imaginary line from the prints, we descended to a thick clump of bushes about which the mud had been roiled as by a struggle.

At one point something wide and heavy had been dragged toward the shrubbery. My flash beam followed the broad trail into the bushes. A boy's face sprang into view.

And the pattern became right.

He crouched on his side, wedged among the gnarled branches. A boy of about twenty, possibly younger. His tongue and eyes protruded. Purple welts spotted his bare throat.

"That's what she's scared of," Carson breathed, kneeling at my side to peer at the boy. "She's been two-timing her old man. It's like the others after all. We crawl in, Cap'n?"

"Homicide crawls in," I told him, rising.

I left him there to guard the body, sent Sergeant Murphy to launch the homicide machinery, then had Patrolman Jaffe drive me back to my West End apartment.

It took fifteen minutes on my phone before I could contact Williams, a rookie I had borrowed from Brooklyn.

"I muffed it, Captain," he reported unhappily.

"How?"

"I stayed with Carson until 2:30. He was around the Socony Yacht Basin. You know, on—"

"I know," I cut in. "What happened?"

"He hung around there a while smokin' and lookin' out at the boats. Then he chucked the smoke in the water and started north fast. I had to keep pretty far back because the walk along the river is wide open there. When he turned into the underpass I started runnin', but he was out of sight when I got through it—"

"Think he spotted you?"

"I don't see how, Captain."

"We'll get three more fellows over from Brooklyn tomorrow and keep him boxed. Good night, Williams."

I broke the connection and tried to pick up my interrupted thread of sleep, but thought of Plainclothesman Carson and the case instead.

In four weeks Carson had emerged as my only suspect. Out of eight attacks he had been the first man on the scene five times. In three parks. The odds against such a coincidence were fantastic.

I thought of his preoccupation with sex, the snicker in his voice when he mentioned women, his locker at headquarters lined with nude pin-ups. All blondes.

Like the eight attack victims. All blondes.

A circumstantial basis for suspicion. But all I had.

Newspapers were getting hold of it and the Commissioner was

raging. My park details had been doubled, then tripled. Parks were closed at midnight. Officers patrolled the paths. Radio cars inched along behind probing searchlights. Mounted police explored the off-trail areas.

But neckers scaled fences and avoided paths and ducked low when spotlights floated by, and grew silent when footsteps or horse hooves sounded near.

And where neckers went, the attacker followed. Seeking pretty blondes. On cloudy nights. Only when clouds darkened the night sky. In the past four weeks there had been eight such nights. Eight attacks. Seven boy friends beaten into unconsciousness. And now —a corpse.

"Get him! Get him! Get him!" the Commissioner had roared, pounding his desk.

I had gone to Dr. Rosen, the Bellevue psychiatrist, who told me, "The pattern indicates a compulsive rapist. A man who has been, or fancies he's been, deeply injured by a blonde, probably on a cloudy night. His victims are proxies. He exacts vengeance on her through them."

I had told him, "We have a fellow on a park detail who seems to qualify."

"Married?"

"No. But at home he's dominated by an overblown blonde mother and two blonde sisters. The mother tried to get his pay mailed to her. On two occasions neighbors phoned the local precinct when he got into loud altercations with his sisters."

"Healthy reactions, Captain." Dr. Rosen shrugged. "He fights back. Your rapist doesn't know how. Under normal circumstances he may be the antithesis of your man, avoiding open retaliation against the object of his hatred. Unless you have other evidence, what you told me is hardly a basis for suspicion."

My "other evidence" boiled down to Carson having been first on the scene five out of eight times. I couldn't get that damning statistic out of my mind.

I couldn't get the case out of my mind.

At that, living with it was better than thinking of Martha. Martha's picture was still on my bureau, a blob of dimly reflected night light across from the bed.

I tried to visualize my reactions were Martha to be attacked.

Couldn't. For five weeks my feelings about her had been frozen. Even when she phoned me from Reno two nights earlier, and I heard mockery in her huskily whispered, "Miss me, Bob?"

I couldn't say, because I didn't know.

I had asked, "What do you want?" noting that my voice was dry and incurious. To her it was a fuse.

"Not *you!*"

I had broken the connection, only for the long distance operator to ring a few moments later, bringing me Martha's apologetic: "I'm sorry, Bob. I guess I'm still raw inside. What I want—"

Her tan riding habit. I had sent it the following morning and promptly forgot her again. But now, weighing my attitude, I seemed to be neither glad nor sorry she was getting the divorce. It even took effort to think of her now.

I finally drifted into a troubled sleep. . . .

"Same pattern." Inspector Quinn, of Homicide, shrugged. "He caught 'em neckin' on a bench near the bushes where you found the kid. She finally admitted that much. Her talk of being abducted on upper Broadway was baloney. He must have sneaked up on 'em from behind. She knows nothin' except 'a black thing' hit her head and knocked her cold."

"A black thing?"

"Her words." Quinn smiled wryly. A leather-faced, old-school cop, he did not smile often. "We picked a fleck of black enamel from her hair. The lab says it's off metal."

"How about the boy?"

"Strangled from behind by big, strong hands. Broke the kid's neck."

"Anything else?"

"That shower spoiled any other traces." Quinn scowled, which more became him. "Think that's why he picks cloudy nights?"

"Dr. Rosen thinks it's a fetish because the pattern is always the same. The rapist is exacting a vicarious vengeance against a blonde he associates with a cloudy night. A lover spurned by a blonde, or a two-timed husband, or the son of a dominating blonde mother. His victims are proxies."

"And doxies." Quinn allowed himself a second tight smile, establishing a sort of record. "This one's a blonde wildcat. You want her?"

"Yes."

"Seen her husband?"

I had; a graying man with a big belly. She had been his secretary in a textile converting firm. The dead boy had been a shipping clerk there. The husband intended to get a New York divorce on the grounds of adultery.

"I saw him," I nodded.

"Old enough to have known better," Quinn growled, rising. "If he divorces her she says she'll sue the department. I'll have her sent in."

Carson had been right in one respect. She entered my office as if it were a burlesque runway, with a slow, hip-swaying stride. Sans dirt and freshly groomed, she was not pretty but beautiful, as a cat can be beautiful. Her violet eyes were large and tilted. Her cheeks tapered below high bones to lips that were full and soft, as if poised to kiss. She had platinum hair, piled high.

"Please be seated, Mrs. Jackson. I'm Captain Ryan."

She occupied the chair warily, her eyes and shoulders tense. She wore an aquatone dress of woolen material. Her only jewelry was a heart-shaped locket suspended by a slender golden chain from her neck. Her proportions, as Carson had observed, were startling, but not so startling as the fury in her eyes when mine finally got back to them.

"And they hand out parking tickets!" she stormed in a low, intense voice. I was puzzled.

"Ma'am?"

"For what's on your mind, you ought to get ten years!"

I shuffled reports on my desk stupidly. When I looked up again her fury had given way to curiosity.

"I never thought I'd live to see a blushing cop!"

"Sorry," I murmured.

"A gentleman, too. Didn't I see you last night?"

"In the park, Mrs. Jackson. Now I'm concerned with the possibility that this attacker didn't happen on you accidentally; that he had seen you before and followed you. Possibly where you live, or worked, or shop, or wherever you spend your time. A stranger you may have noticed watching you the past few days. Or someone you know. For instance, a man whose advances you may have repulsed."

A smile chased the last sign of wariness from her face. "You talk like a book."

"My cross, Mrs. Jackson. Now, if you will think—"

"Riffle a phone book," she drawled, a disturbingly familiar expression in her eyes, "and make with a pin."

"Ma'am?"

She shrugged. "Something about me. It brings you running."

"Me?"

"Men. I have to keep brushing you off. Not you, personally. You're not a wolf. Maybe you don't have to be with those shoulders. But you asked me who I might have—repulsed?"

"Yes, Mrs. Jackson."

"That's it. In restaurants, theaters, night clubs, on the street—anywhere I go I keep brushing them off like flies. All the time. All over town. That's why I said if you want a list of repulses, riffle a phone book and make with a pin."

She took a cigarette from her aquatone bag. I flicked my lighter and leaned across the desk. She tried to reach my face with a smoke streamer. It hovered between us.

"How about men you know?" I asked tiredly. My headache was returning.

"Jimmy was all." Her tone softened. "The poor kid."

I let the obituary hang, fingered reports, then asked my next question without looking up.

"I'm grasping for straws, Mrs. Jackson. I know you were knocked unconscious before you could see the man. But there are degrees of unconsciousness, even a twilight zone where impressions are recalled later, much like memories of a dream—"

She remained silent. I stared at the reports, waiting. Her silence continued. I raised my eyes, knowing she was waiting for that. In hers was that same disturbing glint. I recognized it now. Like Martha's eyes in the hospital. Almost mockery. But her voice was thoughtful:

"Yes. Something I remembered when I got up this morning. Like you said. I wasn't sure I'd dreamed it or what. A man whispering the same thing over and over again."

"What thing?"

She kept her eyes on mine and repeated a gutter epithet half a dozen times, concluding, "Like that. You're the blushingest man I ever saw."

"Could you recognize that whisper if you heard it again?"

"Maybe."

"We rounded up eight suspects this morning. There's no point your confronting them, since you didn't see your assailant. But we could bring them behind you one at a time and have them whisper —what he whispered."

She squashed her cigarette in my desk tray, leaving the crimson-smeared tip erect. "Tomorrow?" She frowned. "I'm too jumpy now. What with old Jackson screaming for a divorce—and what happened last night. It left me sort of—" She shrugged, keeping her gaze intent on mine. "What comes between 'Captain' and 'Ryan'?"

"Robert."

"I'll call you Bob. Skip the Mrs. Jackson. When his shysters finish, I'll be Miss Holden again. Sally. I keep a little two-room apartment at 483 West 84th Street under that name. Sally Holden. Apartment 3A. It's all the home I've got now. If I remember anything else about last night—well, you might drop in. If you get any redder, your face will explode."

I couldn't have driven a word through my lips with a mallet.

She came to her feet and smoothed her dress with a slow caress, her eyes intent on mine. Her voice was almost a whisper.

"Be seeing you, Bob?"

I could no more have moved or spoken as she left my office had I been bound to my chair and gagged.

Even less, after the remainder of that office day had blurred past, could I keep my feet from their appointed round.

"That's *all* of it!" Sally wailed from across the room. "I don't remember anything else until that plainclothes cop shook me awake. Bob, is this why you came up here?"

I sat on the divan in the living room-kitchenette of her small apartment feeling my face flame. She eyed me in half-amused exasperation, then came over to sit by my side and put her hand gently on mine.

"Look, Bob. I'm glad you came because I'd have flipped without anyone to talk to. But can't we skip the third degree and talk about something else for a while? Us, for instance?"

"I'm too much of a cop," I began, but I found her lips poised an inch from mine. She eliminated the inch. I became less of a cop. She drew back, smiling.

"That didn't hurt, did it?"

I grinned and fingered her golden locket. I flicked it open. Inside: *Sally and Myron forever*.

"Who's Myron?"

"Was. The kid next door. We were going to elope. He eloped with a mortar shell in Korea instead. So I married old Lardbelly. Then Jimmy came along, looking so much like Myron it hurt. That's my true confession. What's yours?"

"My wife's been in Reno five weeks."

"Who'd she catch you with?"

"A truck caught her. A night she was supposed to be in Mt. Vernon with her mother. She was on the front seat of a Ford sedan parked on a Bronx side street when the truck skidded into it. They had to cut her out of the wreck with torches. She was unconscious. The driver was dead."

"Your best friend, natch."

"A stranger."

"And you let her go to Reno?"

"It's cleaner that way."

"She'll sock you for alimony. That's what Lardbelly's scared of, why he wants a New York divorce."

"No alimony. She signed an agreement."

"What's she like?"

"A long-legged blonde like you. We met at a church dance."

"She nice?"

"No."

"Because she played around?"

"Yes."

"Am I nice?"

"Yes."

"Make sense."

"You're honest. She pretended to a virtue she didn't have."

The inch between our lips disappeared again, spurting my blood pressure, unhardening my arteries, turning the hair at my temples from gray to black again.

She drew back with a breathless laugh. "Just thought of something funny. I'm practically attacking the cop who's chasing the animal who attacked me. Like a merry-go-round—"

My headache returned like the blow of a fist. I got to my feet and strode to the window and stared down blindly at 84th Street.

"What is it, Bob?" she whispered, coming up behind me. "I put my foot in my mouth?"

I shook my head at her dim reflection in the glass. "My fault, Sally. I just hadn't thought of it like that. I wanted your company so desperately—"

"Wanted?"

"Still do." I forced a smile through my frown in the glass. "We'll pick it up tomorrow, or the day after. I'm too much of a cop; I take my job too seriously, they tell me. I used to work myself sick on Homicide. This is more of the same. As if it's a contest to the death between the man who attacked you and myself. The mere thought of him sickens me."

She came between me and the window, standing so close I could smell her blondeness, like the scent of an open field.

"Good-bye, Bob?"

"Of course not! Just good night."

Her long scarlet-tipped fingers smoothed the graying hair at my temples.

"You're a funny guy, Bob. You're built like a dock walloper, got the face of a priest. And inside you're like a high school kid on his first date. I'm nuts about you."

"I'm a funny guy."

"You better see me again."

"Yes."

"You don't, I'll come down to Centre Street and pick up from here right in your own office. You hear me, you big baboon?"

The phone awakened me at one in the morning. For a few moments I lay in bed, confused. The night sky outside my window was flecked with stars. In four weeks these had been my first hours of freedom from nightmares about the case. I owed that to Sally.

But a starlit sky made the pattern wrong. I groped for the phone, heard a long-distance operator, and felt myself freeze.

Martha came on with her little girl's voice: "Bob, I'm broke."

"I gave you $4,000. All I had. You've only been there five weeks."

"I know, Bob. I've been bad. I was winning at first. I'd planned to send you back the $4,000. But then the system went kaput."

I could hear music and voices in the background. And an urgent whisper. As if someone was prompting her.

My headache returned. I asked, "What system?"

"Well, this cowboy I met told me—"

Percentage—the god of every ex-gambling Bowery stiff. A law-of-averages system. As if each deck of cards and each roulette wheel had built into it the parabolic law of chance.

"It worked for five weeks, Bob. But then—"

The law of averages was repealed until she went broke.

"I'll scrape up $500 in the morning, Martha. That should see you through. If it doesn't, and you fail to go through with the divorce, I'll file for one here in New York."

I broke the connection before she could reply. My headache was raging. I couldn't return to sleep. I lit a reading lamp, got into my big chair with duplicates of the case reports, and tried to fathom a new lead from the Whisperer's pattern of attack.

But my thoughts kept drifting back to the Saturday night Sergeant Murphy had phoned me about Martha.

She had been extricated from the wreck by the time I got there. I stood in the drizzle looking through the jagged hole in the Ford's jammed door at the corpse of the man still inside. The steering shaft had impaled him. A blond man in a gray suit. A stranger. A total stranger.

It was with her little girl's voice that she had spoken to me from her hospital bed. "Can't I make it up to you some way, Bob?"

"Yes," I had told her, surprised that I felt no emotion looking down at her, no emotion at all. "Get a Reno divorce. No alimony. I'll send your things. You're not to set foot in my apartment again."

And then mockery had filled her eyes and voice. "Why, you prissy old maid! Do you think he was the *first*? You think any red-blooded woman would stay satisfied, married to a dull inhibited—"

The rest followed me down the long corridor in hoarse screams

I walked into the night. And kept walking through endless drizzle. Until I found myself awakening in my own bed, trembling.

Plainclothesman Carson relished the assignment. I had him stand in the interrogation room's doorway and several times whisper the gutter epithet, ostensibly to show the suspects how.

Eight of them. Netted around Riverside Drive between the time of Sally's attack and dawn. Three park-bench sleepers, four strollers who claimed to be insomniacs, and a huge dock worker whose frenzied incoherence earmarked him for observation in Bellevue when the experiment was over.

Sally's back was to the doorway as the eight men, following Carson's example, appeared behind her and whispered the epithet. When it was over, Sally could only shift a wry smile from Inspector Quinn to me and say, "I couldn't even tell one from another. It's impossible."

"It is," Quinn agreed. "Sorry to have taken up your time, Mrs. Jackson."

Her eyes questioned mine as Carson began to escort her out. I watched the tremor in his big, freckled hand reaching for her arm, then turned to find Inspector Quinn regarding me with amusement. When the door closed behind them, he murmured, "What you got on Carson?"

"Carson?"

Quinn snorted. "He could have briefed 'em downstairs. You had her test his voice along with the others. Why?"

"He was first on the scene five times."

"What else?"

"He's powerful, over six feet, and sex-obsessed."

"I thought this fiend hates women."

"One woman. Others, only when they remind him of her. And only during spells. Assuming he's schizophrenic."

"What else?"

"Carson is smothered under women at home. His mother and two sisters are all big, loud, domineering blondes."

"What else?"

"I keep going back to his being first on the scene five times. In three different parks. We switch assignments nightly so prowlers won't get used to our men. The odds against one officer running into five out of eight victims under such conditions are fantastic."

"Been tailin' him?"

"We lost him just before Sally—Mrs. Jackson—was attacked. Yesterday I borrowed three more rookies from Brooklyn, making four in all. They're to lie in wait wherever his patrol will be the next cloudy night."

"Tonight," Quinn grunted. "Accordin' to the papers."

"Tonight, then. And every cloudy night from now on. Until we're sure one way or the other."

We spent the rest of the afternoon checking my dragnet.

My men had rounded up all former sex offenders, checked psycho discharges from hospitals, prisons, the armed services. No lead had been found.

I had used maps in an effort to find a geographical pattern. But the Whisperer struck at random. His victims and their boy friends came from widely separated parts of the city. The only pattern we had was that he struck from behind on cloudy or drizzly nights— and concentrated on blondes.

We checked my decoy set-up: blonde policewomen paired with plainclothesmen and sent into the parks on cloudy nights. And my pattern of patrols varied from night to night, men and routes being shifted nightly.

We reread the eight attack reports and, in the end, could do little more than stare at each other.

"One thing," Quinn finally growled. "It's almost as if this guy anticipates you. He always attacks when the nearest patrol is moving away from the scene."

"I keep thinking of Carson."

"Or dumb luck." Quinn shrugged. "Ten times this many patrols couldn't locate all the neckers in all the parks on any one night."

We left it at that.

The moisture-weighted atmosphere, when I finally left my office, depressed me. I walked out of an upper Broadway restaurant unable to recall what I had eaten. Too unsettled to return home, entered a movie house—and emerged fifteen minutes later with headache and no idea of what the picture was supposed to be about.

Back in the apartment the phone was ringing.

Sally.

"You looked so grim down at headquarters, darling."

"It's a grim place."

She laughed. "Well, I've got the cure for that. Scotch, rye, and bourbon. And if that doesn't wear down your resistance, I'll use a blackjack. Coming soon?"

"Not this evening, Sally. A cloudy sky is forecast."

"Oh? . . . *oh?*" A pause for reflection. Then: "Kit wants to date me. Shall I?"

"Who?"

"Carson. He says all his friends call him Kit. Didn't you know that?"

"I know him as Martin Henry Carson. Tonight?"

"With Stoneface keeping him up all day to breathe nasty language down my neck?" Her laughter was low and delicious. "I shouldn't rat on him, but Stoneface is what they call you, darling. Anyhow, he has to be at work midnight, doesn't he?"

"Yes. Will you date him?"

"I'm asking you."

"I can't decide, Sally. On the one hand I'd like your reactions to the man when his guard is down; on the other, you may run into trouble."

"What could happen that didn't?"

"The same would be terrible enough. I'd have men covering you. But a cornered man may act desperately. The decision must be yours."

"All right. He's off tomorrow. He asked me to go dancing. I will."

"Good."

"*Good?* Aren't you jealous?"

I didn't know. Probably not. Sally as an instrument for trapping Carson seemed more desirable at the moment than Sally as a substitute for Martha.

The sense of these musings must have reached her, because I heard her try to slam the connection, miss, mutter *"Damn!"* and try again. This time she succeeded.

My phone rang immediately. Long distance. Martha. Screaming: "Bob? I've been haunting the telegraph office all day! They must think I'm crazy. You promised—"

I had forgotten about the $500.

"I'm sorry Martha. Tomorrow morning—"

"What will I do *now?* You go and wire it immediately! Bob? Bob, do you hear me—?"

They could hear her in Canarsie. I couldn't get hold of $500 at this hour. In the morning I would negotiate a bank loan. I didn't tell her that. I told her nothing. My head throbbed. I broke the connection and went to the bathroom for aspirins.

When the pain subsided I took her photo off the bureau and studied her pale blonde, aristocratic face. I thought of her well-bred manner, her charm, her tenderness.

A year and a half of that. No violent passions had disturbed our marriage. It had seemed to burn along with a quiet, small flame.

Too quiet, too small, apparently, for her.

So a truck skidded out of control on wet pavement and they dragged her from the embrace of a corpse. . . .

I flung her picture at the radiator and watched its frame spring open. Splinters of glass flew. I wrenched my gaze from her delicate smile on the floor up to the window. Low, black clouds were beginning to swarm into the night sky.

My phone was ringing. I had been dozing in the big chair. Lieutenant Gold was on the line.

"An attack, Captain. Fifteen-year-old girl on East River Drive."

My watch said 11:30. The pattern was all wrong. Lieutenant Gold's voice went on:

"We got three of 'em."

"Three?"

"Teen-agers. Call themselves the Arrows. Nine in all. Want our men to round up the other six?"

Outside my window the night was almost pitch-black.

"No, Lieutenant. Let the local precinct handle it. Keep all our men in the parks."

"Yessir."

I stood at my living-room window looking down on West End Avenue. Some pedestrians carried umbrellas under their arms. It wasn't raining, just threatening.

I thought of sleep, decided I couldn't. And thought of Sally. kept thinking of Sally. Her boldness had both stimulated and re pelled me. But the gentleness below her brassy surface had affected me deeply. I dialed her number, then listened to her bell ring on and off a full minute, unanswered.

Carson?

Sergeant Murphy's voice was hoarse in the receiver. He had just checked in. Morning hoarseness fifteen minutes to midnight. He said, "I'll see, Captain." I listened to headquarters noises, then: "Carson didn't check in yet."

"Let me know when he does."

"Right."

It took a few minutes to locate Carson's home number. Before I could dial it, mine rang again. Sergeant Murphy again:

"Carson just checked in. Want to talk to him?"

"No, Sergeant."

My hand left a wet trace on the receiver. So she wasn't with Carson. Out somewhere. Possibly at a movie, or a friend's house, or with another man. My fault. She *had* invited me. I found my image grinning ruefully back at me from the bathroom mirror as I swallowed another pair of aspirins.

My headache eased a little and I crawled into bed and tried to sleep, and did.

And found Sally.

In my doorway. She wore a transparent raincoat over her aquatone dress, a transparent hood over her platinum halo. She was smiling.

Not at me. At someone behind me.

Turning, I saw only my living room.

Turning back, the doorway was empty. I stepped through it and saw Sally moving down the corridor slowly, her skirt swishing from side to side in languorous counterpoint to the click of her high heels.

I ran down the corridor, trying to call her back. But something had happened to my voice. I ran into the elevator after her.

As it descended she tilted her lips to me, her eyes sparkling. I couldn't respond. I wanted to. My lips approached hers eagerly. At the point of contact hers vanished.

Sally vanished.

I seemed enmeshed in fog. I groped through it and emerged into a cloud-darkened night scene. Vaguely familiar. Before me

curved an ascending sidewalk flanked by a low stone fence to my
left and empty benches to the right. About a hundred yards ahead,
walking slowly away from me, was Sally.

Occasional headlights, coming and going, swam past to my
right.

Riverside Drive.

I must have awakened partially then, because I recall becoming
aware of my heart hammering against my ribs like a fist. I remember trying to open my eyes, being unable to, struggling desperately
to open them—and finally succeeding. I glimpsed a kaleidoscope
of shadows. Then back to the scene on Riverside Drive.

Sally was gone. I stared around at the rows of benches, the motionless trees, the empty sidewalk. I ran to the low wall and
peered over it. In the shadows below I saw Sally picking herself
off the grass.

I vaulted the wall and floated gently down. Too gently. Too
slowly. By the time I landed Sally was moving away again, keeping to tree shadows, avoiding lawns and park walks where occasional lamps blurred the darkness.

Fear gripped me as I recognized the direction she was taking.
But my feet had become rooted. I stared about wildly, seeking
help, and saw nothing but empty benches along the paths, empty
lawns spreading away into the night. I tried to remember which
patrol I had assigned to this area. I couldn't remember.

Dreaming. I knew I was dreaming. I had a vague impulse to
force myself awake, use my phone, get help. I couldn't. I just
couldn't.

And then I faced Sally again. Near the KEEP OFF THE GRASS
sign. She was smiling, unbuckling her raincoat. Deliberately she
bunched it up, then flared it like a curtain between us. When it de
scended she was gone.

*The boy was there! Tongue and eyes protruding. Purple welt
on his neck. The same boy—Jimmy. Standing. Facing me with
bulging, dead eyes. The same boy! The same boy!*

My head was one roaring scream. I seized it. I pounded it with
my fists. I rolled with the agony, sobbed in relief when it began to
pass.

My eyes opened and I stared at Sally. Not the boy. Sally was
standing there. I stared at her golden locket. *Sally and Myron for
ever.*

I stared at Sally. She stared back as if I were a stranger. Her lips were moving but I heard no words. Her eyes were widening. They were widening, widening.

Blotted by shadow.

I could hear her through it. Screaming. She was screaming.

I could stand no more. I heard myself moan, and opened my eyes.

I was in my own bed, bathed in sweat from head to toe. The phone was ringing steadily on my night table. My head ached, my tongue felt thick and fuzzy. The phone shrilled with the same urgent regularity of Sally's screams. My hand trembled reaching for it.

Sergeant Murphy, his voice unsteady:

"It's the worst yet, Captain. I'm sending Jaffe around with the car."

My stomach was a knot. I felt cold; covered with sweat, but cold. I could barely croak into the instrument: "Where?"

"Same place. Can you beat it!"

"Where?"

"Riverside Park. The exact same place. Not only that, Captain, but—"

Every nerve in my body jumped. "Dammit, Sergeant! But what?"

"The same girl!"

I sat staring at the dead instrument in my hand. It was fantastic, frightening. How, in my dream, had I known it was Sally? How had I known it was the same place? If, when I got there, I learned she had actually worn a transparent raincoat, how could that be explained? My head throbbed with unanswerable questions.

My body ached with fatigue. As if I had not been asleep from midnight to dawn, but had actually been out in the night running after Sally.

Even my damp clothes on the floor added to the illusion. Drizzle blowing in through my open window, of course.

I began to dress, thinking of Martha. Later I would borrow the 500 and wire it to her and that would finish it.

I was getting into my raincoat when Patrolman Jaffe rang the downstairs bell.

This time Sally was not defiant. No need for an intern to wheel her into an ambulance. She did not scream at Sergeant Murphy or concoct a false story of being abducted on upper Broadway.

I stopped the moving litter, then raised an edge of the canvas and looked at the blood splotch that had been Sally's forehead, but not seeing it; seeing, instead, the edge of the transparent raincoat they had folded over her.

The litter moved on and into the waiting morgue van. I turned. Inspector Quinn was gripping my arm. His face was ashen in the dawn light.

"Filthy, isn't it, Bob? The same girl. The same place—"

"The same man?"

Incredulity distorted his face. "If it was, she knew him. She knew him but wasn't afraid of him. She knew him, but not that he was the guy who'd attacked her before. At least that narrows the field."

I beckoned to Sergeant Murphy. Quinn waved him back.

"Carson?"

I nodded.

"No dice. You had him in Morningside Park all night. I checked him first thing. Carson was under observation every minute of his tour. He still is. You got to know her, Bob. Who might have been able to get that close to her?"

"Husband?"

"Checked him also."

"She said, 'Riffle a phone book and make with a pin.' "

"Oh, great!"

"I was planning to bait her with Carson."

"She get under your skin?"

"Deep."

Deeper than I had suspected. I could hear her whispering *You're a funny guy, Bob. You're built like a dock walloper, go the face of a priest. And inside you're like a high school kid o his first date. I'm nuts about you.*

But she went to the park with a two-legged beast. She soug romance. New thrills. New sensations. Like getting her forehea smashed.

"Bob," Inspector Quinn shook my arm, "you're dead on yo feet. Have Jaffe take you home. I'll cover for you downtown. T morrow we'll go over the whole picture once more."

I did not realize I had submitted to his suggestion until r

apartment door closed behind me. In the foyer I slowly got out of my raincoat. It slipped to the floor. As I picked it up, my flash rolled from a pocket—and something else.

I frowned down at it a long while before stooping and raising it by a broken end of slender golden chain. Sally's locket. *Sally and Myron forever.* Dirt-caked. I couldn't remember picking it up at the scene, but I must have. How else could it have got into my pocket? I would turn it in tomorrow.

My flash must have dropped from my pocket at the scene also. It was caked with drying reddish grime. I couldn't recall dropping it, couldn't remember how bits of its enamel had come to be chipped off.

I spent most of the day at my desk writing this record of everything that has happened since I first laid eyes on Sally. I have included so many personal details—including my nightmare—because seemingly unrelated memories are often linked.

And something seems to have emerged. I sense it.

But my brain is dull. I cannot find it. Something, I feel, having to do with the attacker's pattern.

Not Carson. That much is certain now. Happening on the scene five out of eight times *was* a coincidence.

All I know of the man I'm looking for is that he is big, powerful; that he was injured by some blonde on a cloudy night; and that, either by luck or plan, he attacks when the nearest patrol is moving away.

And something else. I sense that important knowledge of him and his pattern is hidden somewhere in this account. But the words blur. My brain is dull, fogged. I am very tired now. Almost tired enough to sleep.

I will show this to Inspector Quinn in the morning. Maybe he can discover what I can only sense. Something that may lead us to the attacker.

I hope so, I fervently hope so.

From the 1955 anthology . . .

You may have wondered what can turn a once exemplary man into something far less, or what can become of the pure and unbending standards of an aspiring politician. On occasion you may yourself have found—which of us has not?—that the wisdom of the moment dictated that compromise should rescue you in a ticklish spot. You may, like me, find Richard Deming's tale more than a little sobering in its wider implications.

RICHARD DEMING

The Choice

The thing I want to get across is that I'm an honest man. In all my years of public service I've never accepted a dishonest cent.

In most other respects too I think I'm what society calls a "good citizen." I'm a kind father and a good husband. I'm active in church and community affairs. And even beyond that, I've devoted my whole life to public service.

At the moment I serve as district attorney of St. Michael County.

In case my stressing of my respectability gives you the idea I am building up to confessing some crime, I'd better explain that I'm not. I don't want to create a false impression. I merely have a choice to make.

No matter how I choose I'll remain a solid and respected citizen. If I choose one way, I can look forward to spending the rest of my life pleasantly but unexcitingly in private law practice, probably at a better income than my salary as district attorney.

I choose the other way, almost certainly I will be my state's next governor and possibly, though I admit improbably, even end my political career in the White House.

The only way I can explain my position is to say I drifted into it. Each compromise with my moral precepts seemed so small at the time, and the consequences of not compromising seemed so drastic, even now when I look back I can't honestly blame myself.

I can't really blame the System either, for that would merely be blaming all humanity.

My first contact with what I have come to think of as the "System" was over the Max Bloom case, when I was a green young assistant district attorney. I was twenty-six at the time, and the junior of eight assistants.

Max Bloom was a bookie, and there was nothing exceptional about the case. Two officers had raided his bookshop, caught Max in the act of accepting bets and placed him under arrest. Since there seemed to be no possible defense, I contemplated a single appearance in court, where the defendant undoubtedly would plead guilty and accept the usual fine.

Instead, Big Joey Martin dropped in to see me.

I knew who Big Joey was, though I had never before met him. He was political boss of the Sixth and Seventh Wards, and also reputed to have some sort of connection with organized gambling. He was a huge man, at least six feet four and weighing probably two hundred and seventy pounds. Some of this was muscle, but a good deal of it was plain fat.

He came into my cubbyhole office without knocking, carefully lowered himself into a chair, squirmed until he was comfortable and began fanning himself with his hat.

"You George Kenneday?" he asked when these preliminaries were over.

I nodded.

"I guess you know who I am."

I nodded again. "Joey Martin."

For a moment or two the fat man merely fanned himself with his hat. Then he said, "They tell me you got the prosecution against Maxie Bloom."

I nodded for the third time.

"Somebody slipped up. It ain't Maxie's turn for two more months, and he's sorer than hell about losing two weeks' business.

I tried to tell him I'd get his next tumble postponed two months overtime, but I can't talk no sense into his head. He's kind of a psycho, you know. I'm afraid he'll blow his lid in court and start yammering to the judge about getting his protection money back. So I think we better work out a dismissal or something."

I looked at the man with my mouth open. "Are you asking me to drop charges against a lawbreaker?"

"A lawbreaker?" Joey Martin repeated in a surprised tone. "Maxie's a bookie, not no criminal." He eyed me narrowly, then said, "I ain't asking you nothing if you're going to get horsey about it. I guess I just took it for granted you knew the setup. Forget I bothered you."

Heaving himself to his feet, he nodded indifferently and ambled out of my office. And I was so flabbergasted by the whole performance, I just sat there open-mouthed and watched him go.

Fifteen minutes later I was called into the office of First Assistant District Attorney Clark Gleason.

"How are you, George?" Gleason said in a friendly voice, waving me to a chair. "Beginning to get the feel of things?"

I told him I was getting along fine.

"Reason I called you in, George, I'm taking over the Max Bloom case myself. Mind dropping the folder next time you pass my office?"

Carefully I folded my hands in my lap. "Has Joey Martin been to see you, Mr. Gleason?"

"Well, yes. As a matter of fact, he just left."

"I see. Mr. Gleason, only a few minutes ago Joey Martin practically ordered me to get Bloom's charge dismissed. He said something about protection money and that Bloom's arrest had been a mistake in timing on the part of the police. When I started to jump him, he seemed more surprised than alarmed, and walked out. Now I learn he's been to see you, and you're taking over Bloom's case. I think I'm entitled to an explanation."

Gleason examined me thoughtfully for a long time before answering. Eventually he asked, "Why do you think I'm taking over the case?"

I said with a mixture of caution and belligerence, "I must be mistaken, Mr. Gleason, but on the surface it looks as though the office takes orders from a two-bit racketeer."

Gleason's smile was rueful, but it didn't contain any anger

"This office doesn't take orders from anyone, George. But sometimes we have to do political favors. Do you know who Joey Martin is?"

"Sure. A professional gambler."

"A little more than that George. Joey is the boy who delivers the votes down in the Sixth and Seventh Wards. All the votes. Election after election he turns out a solid majority for the party. In return he occasionally asks a small favor. Never much of a favor and never very often. It's just practical politics to go along when he asks."

"Even if you have to violate your oath of office?"

"Oh, for cripes sake, George," Gleason said impatiently. "Max Bloom isn't a murderer or bank robber. Everybody knows bookshops are tolerated in St. Michael and what raids are made are only token raids. Two weeks after his trial Max would be back in business in the same spot even if we got a conviction."

I said, "What you're saying in effect is that this office knows the police deliberately protect illegal bookshops. Even that they accept protection money for it. Yet we condone it because it wouldn't be practical politics to crack down. Why doesn't the D.A. swear out warrants for everybody concerned, including a few crooked cops?"

"Because next election there would be a new district attorney. If you intend to follow a political career, George, now is as good a time as any to learn the hard facts of political life. We're aware that the police to some extent connive with Joey and his kind, and we don't approve of it. But attempting to stop it would be tilting at windmills. No one in this office has any direct connection with men like Joey and no one receives any payoff. But as a matter of practical politics we sometimes have to rub the backs of such men, because it's the votes controlled by ward leaders like Joey Martin that keep our party in power. Call it a violation of public trust if you want, but what's the alternative? Kicking Joey out of the office and having two wards refuse to back John Doud for D.A. in the next primary?"

"Your job and mine aren't elective," I said. "We're appointed."

"By the D.A.," Gleason agreed. "Whose job is elective. And you're only kidding yourself if you think your appointment was entirely on merit. Weren't you sponsored by someone?"

Reluctantly I admitted, "My Uncle Crosby is an alderman."

When I left Gleason's office there was no question in my mind that the whole system was wrong in spite of the first assistant D.A.'s glib argument about practical politics. But I couldn't think of anywhere to go with a complaint. It would have been silly to go to the police, who seemed to be a party to the arrangement. And just as silly to expect action from the D.A. or any other elected official who owed allegiance to the System.

In the end I did nothing, justifying myself by deciding I would have taken some kind of action if I had been asked to get Max Bloom a dismissal myself. But since the case had been taken out of my hands, there really wasn't any action I could take.

Looking back, I still can't see anything I could have done. I have come to regard the Max Bloom case as the first compromise with my principles, but in a way it wasn't a compromise at all. At least not in an active sense. All I actually did was accept a situation about which I could do nothing. How many sincerely honest men in the same position would have done anything else?

Would you have?

It was nearly four years before I was called upon to make the next big compromise, though in the meantime I found myself making more and more small ones. Even now I can't put my finger on any one point of my career and say, "Here is where I should have resisted," because it was a gradual process. The mere mental act of accepting the System as a necessary evil of politics opened the way for greater and greater departures from what I knew to be right.

Yet if I had the chance to live this period over, I know my reactions would be the same. There was no fighting the System. Either you conformed, or you retired to private life. And since the party had begun to regard me as a bright young man with a political future, I conformed.

My growing influence in local party affairs was largely the result of the reputation I was gaining as a prosecutor. Actually this reputation was based almost entirely on a single murder case which the papers seemed to think I handled with some brilliance but the party didn't care about that. What counted was that I had the public's confidence. As a result when Clark Gleason resigned to accept a job in the State's Attorney's office, I was appointed first assistant district attorney in his place.

During this four years I learned a lot about how the System operated. For the most part what Clark Gleason had told me was quite true. Most elected officials were honest men who had no direct connection with the underworld-controlled political machine which maintained them in office. Yet the influence of ward leaders such as Joey Martin was tremendous. In return for the votes necessary to elect them, officials usually found it expedient to wink at the illegal side activities of Joey and his kind, and occasionally grant favors which came close to criminal conspiracy.

At the time I was appointed first assistant district attorney I hadn't held, or even run for, any elective office, but I was aware of hints within the party that I might make a good district attorney when old John Doud finally decided to retire. I kept these hints alive by actively engaging in party affairs, which brought me in frequent contact with local political bosses.

With an eye on my future, I deliberately cultivated friendly relations with these men, with the result that I was asked for a lot of minor favors. For example, Willie Tamm, president of the Dock Workers' Local and also party leader of the three wards in the dock area, routinely mailed me his traffic tickets to have fixed.

Many similar minor favors were asked of me, but the one big favor I performed was done tacitly without being mentioned by anyone. This was a passive favor. It was simply closing my eyes to the rackets going on in the districts run by the men who controlled the votes.

That is, this was my one big favor prior to the evening Timothy Grange called at my house.

Tim Grange ranked higher both politically and in the underworld than Big Joey Martin. He owned the wire service which brought horse race results into town from all over the country, and his business was leasing this service to individual bookies. He also controlled the party organization for the entire East Side, including the two wards run by Joey Martin.

Grange was one of the men whose friendship I had been deliberately cultivating, but aside from passing time with him at a number of political rallies, we hadn't had much contact prior to the Friday evening he unexpectedly showed up at my house.

He was a tall, slim man in his late forties with iron-gray hair. He arrived about nine o'clock, after both the children were in bed. When he rather nervously refused Mary's offer of a drink with a statement that he had urgent business with me, she went into another room and left us alone in the front room. Grange stated his business at once.

"My kid's in a jam, George. Tim Junior. He's killed a man."

The abruptness of it startled me. "My God!" I said. "Murder?"

He shook his head in nervous impatience. "A traffic accident. He ran over a pedestrian at Fourth and Locust about an hour ago. An old man named Abraham Swartz. I just checked with City Hospital, and the man's dead."

"Oh," I said, partially relieved that it wasn't as serious as I first thought. "Was it Tim's fault?"

Grange paced up and down a moment before answering. Then he said, "He says he wasn't speeding. At least not much. He claims he was going about thirty-five in a thirty-mile zone when this Swartz suddenly stepped from the curb right in front of him."

"I see. Then what are you upset about? It's unfortunate, but those things . . ."

"He didn't stop," George interrupted. "He raced home and hid the car in the garage. Fortunately I happened to be going out just as he came in, and when I saw how upset he was, I forced the story out of him." He paused, then added in a flat voice, "He was drunk."

For a moment I just looked at him. Then I walked over to stare angrily out the window. When I turned again, I said, "At the risk of hurting your feelings, Grange, young Tim is a damned fool."

"I knew that before I came, George. The kid panicked. What's he up against?"

"Manslaughter, probably," I said bluntly. "The combination of hit-and-run and drunken driving almost automatically means a manslaughter charge, no matter whose fault the accident was."

"He's not drunk now. I threw him in a cold shower, and when I left I had my wife pouring black coffee in him."

I said, "The police make a blood test for alcohol content. It's routine in hit-and-run cases. Even if you have him walking straight and talking coherently, they'll be able to judge how drunk he was at the time of the accident."

"Suppose they didn't find him till tomorrow?"

I looked at him. "He can't wait till tomorrow. He'll have to turn himself in at once. If he turns in voluntarily, he may just pos sibly scrape out of the manslaughter charge. But it's already too late for him to get out of the hit-and-run. The law requires any driver involved in an accident to stop immediately and identify himself either to the other party involved or to the police. The law allows the alternate procedure of reporting directly to the nearest police station, but young Tim didn't do that either. The kid is in a jam, and the longer he waits before turning in, the worse the jam is going to get."

"Suppose he reported to the station closest to Fourth and Locust now, George? It was only a little over an hour ago."

"It might as well be a year. The law says immediately."

"Couldn't the report be . . . set back a little?"

I said, "Are you asking me to get the police to falsify a report? This isn't like fixing a parking ticket. Manslaughter is a felony."

"But it's only technically manslaughter," Grange said in a reasonable tone. "If he'd stopped, he wouldn't be in any particular trouble. Manslaughter's kind of a tough rap just for getting panicky."

"Death is kind of a tough rap just for stepping off a curb."

"I'm not excusing the kid, George. But he *is* my kid. I know you're hounded for favors by every ward heeler in town, but I've never asked you for one before. I'll put it right on the line. Get my kid out of this and I'm your friend for life."

He didn't put it into words, but his tone meant I would have the solid backing of the entire East Side any time I wanted to run for any office at all. It also meant I could count on its solid opposition if I failed to help his son.

I think I would have thrown him out of the house if he had offered me money. Even if he had come right out in the open and used his political influence as a weapon, I think I might have turned him down. But he offered me nothing but his friendship, and let the rest dangle there by inference.

There wasn't any middle course I could take. I couldn't, like Pilate, wash my hands of the whole affair. For if I refused to help young Tim out of his jam, I was going to have to prosecute him.

I thought about the talk within the party about my replacing old John Doud when he finally got around to retiring, and realized that with Tim Grange behind me, I wouldn't have to wait for his retirement. I could have the job at the next election.

But not if I refused Timothy Grange. If I insisted on trying his son for manslaughter, from the moment of that decision I could forget all political ambition.

Going to the phone, I dialed the Fourth Street Precinct House, got hold of the night captain, who happened to owe me a favor, and arranged for the log book to show that Timothy Grange Jr. had reported there five minutes after the accident at Fourth and Locust and that he'd been checked and found cold sober.

Conspiracy to compound a felony? Of course it was. But you tell me what else I could have done.

In the nearly eight years that I have been district attorney of St. Michael County I've thought back on this incident often. From the standpoint of abstract justice I admit there is no defense for my action. I was pledged to uphold the law impartially, and in my own mind I know that if Tim Grange Jr. hadn't been the son of an influential politician, I would have prosecuted him for manslaughter.

Yet I can't blame myself for deciding as I did. Kicking the elder Grange out of my house would have accomplished nothing but ending my political career. It wouldn't have brought the dead man back to life.

I can't blame Timothy Grange Sr. for bringing pressure to save his son. What normal father wouldn't? I've decided that if anything is to blame, it's the bad luck which created an impossible situation.

Nevertheless I recognize my action as the first great compromise with my principles. I also recognize that once having made this major step, future compromises became easier and easier.

This was just as well for my peace of mind, for from the moment I was elected district attorney I found it necessary to make more and more compromises. But I was no longer under constant pressure to perform minor favors. This nuisance now fell to my new first assistant, a young man named Edmund Rowe, who as chief prosecutor for the county was in closer contact with both the police and those on the other side of the law than I was.

This was because the district attorney of a county including a large a metropolitan area as St. Michael is a policy maker rather than a courtroom lawyer. He has too many administrative duties to handle prosecutions personally. His concern is crime in a general sense. Specific crimes are the business of his assistants, and had eight to relieve me of this responsibility. Even important cases were tried by Edmund Rowe.

The compromises I was now forced to make came from my policy-making power. And this power was considerable.

At any time after I assumed office I could have eliminated any racket I chose from St. Michael simply by issuing an order to the police. The police wouldn't have liked it, but even though they were to some extent in partnership with the racketeers, they wouldn't have dared to refuse cooperation. The constant dread of any crooked cop is a shake-up in the police department, and the moment a crusading district attorney turns on the heat, every cop, even on a crooked force, becomes a crusader too.

I was aware of my power before I ever assumed office, and I gave a lot of thought to just how I was going to use it. If I wanted to conduct a crusade, I had four years to do it and nothing but the next election could put me out of office. Undoubtedly I could clean up the city and keep it clean during that four years.

But just as undoubtedly I would never again be my party's candidate for any office whatever.

The alternative to fighting crime as I was sworn to do was no longer as simple as it had been when I was merely first assistant district attorney. Then I had been forced to close my eyes to many of the things going on around me, but my cooperation with the underworld had been merely passive. My role had been that of chief public prosecutor, and I lacked the policy-making power of the district attorney.

But now my cooperation had to become active if I was going to cooperate at all. As D.A. it was not enough merely to ignore the rackets controlled by local political bosses. I was now in a spot where I either had to fight racketeering or help cover it up.

For example I often met with volunteer citizens' groups formed to combat organized crime. Sporadically such groups rise in every metropolitan community, and since they usually represent segments of the independent group, they can't just be brushed aside. It's only practical politics to avoid arousing unnecessary resentment in representatives of the Chamber of Commerce, Rotary International and other business groups out of which citizens' committees arise.

Consequently it was necessary to go through the motions of running cleanup drives against gambling, vice and other rackets whenever such a group offered its services. I had a standard procedure for handling such groups.

First I would make a public declaration of war against racketeers. Next my office and the police jointly would release to the papers that citywide raids had taken place and large numbers of arrests had been made. Actually probably a half dozen bookies and an equal number of house madams, all thoughtfully tipped off in advance of the raids, would be dragged in and booked. But since about six cases in addition to the routine parade of drunks and traffic violators was all police court could handle in one day, this was enough to keep a steady stream going before the judge for at least two days. Any of the citizens' groups interested enough to follow up as far as the courtroom usually tired after one day of watching and went away satisfied that justice was being done.

The newspapers, too, occasionally ran editorial campaigns against organized crime in St. Michael, and again it would be necessary to simulate ruthless war against racketeers. In either event, I became so adept, I actually began to gain something of a reputation as a crusading district attorney.

Never once did Timothy Grange or any other racketeer openly ask for this sort of protection. And never once during my entire political career was I ever on the payroll of any racketeer. I cooperated solely to weld a solid voting force behind me.

I succeeded too. When I was elected for my second term as district attorney, I got the most overwhelming majority in the history of St. Michael politics. And that thumping majority put me in line for at least consideration as the party's gubernatorial candidate in the following election.

My hope was only for consideration up to the time Tony Manetti and Arnold Price got interested in me. It is one thing to have the solid political support of a single county, and a different proposition to get an entire state behind you. But after Tim Grange brought Manetti and Price to see me, I began to think of my nomination for governor as almost a certainty. Which, in our one-party state, is the same as election.

This meeting, like my previous one with Grange, took place at my home instead of at my office. Both men were from out of state, Tony Manetti from New York and Arnold Price from Chicago but they both represented the same organization.

Their organization was the national crime syndicate.

Tony Manetti was a squat, swarthy man with heavy features and kinky, close-cropped hair which fitted his head like a skullcap. Arnold Price was tall and lean and slow moving, with gaunt features and the homespun manner of a backwoods farmer.

After the four of us were settled with drinks in the front room and Mary had gone off to another part of the house, Grange opened the conversation.

"I guess you know who Mr. Manetti and Mr. Price are, George," he said. "I been telling them about you, and they thought maybe we ought to have a little political conference." He laughed genially. "You know. Smoke-filled rooms and all that stuff."

Neither man smiled at the joke. Noncommittally I said, "I see."

"As you probably know," Grange went on, "the boys here have been quietly building a political organization throughout the state. Now they're looking around for a candidate to back for governor."

I felt my heart skip a beat. Here, possibly, was the one big break of my career. The backing of a new, but rapidly growing, statewide political machine.

I wasn't for a moment under the impression that syndicate interference in state politics would be a good thing for our state. But neither was I starry-eyed enough to believe anything I did could stop the syndicate's growth. I knew all about what was going on in the state politically, and had accepted it as an undesirable but inevitable development.

Before the arrival of Tony Manetti and Arnold Price in our midst, state politics had been far from clean, but there was little centralization. The two big-city machines, St. Michael's and Tailor City's across the state, were powerful but autonomous units. Numerous smaller but equally autonomous machines ran things in the lesser communities and the rural areas. Though they were all the same party, no one unit was strong enough to dictate statewide policy. State conventions were matters of give and take, with the small rural machines often forming combines strong enough to force through platforms and slates of candidates opposed by both big-city machines.

The syndicate was attempting to weld these divergent groups into a solid, statewide organization whose policy could be controlled from the top. It was common knowledge to the politically informed that Manetti and Price had been spreading huge sums in the form of campaign contributions in the rural areas. It was not so well known that Tailor City had joined forces with the rising new machine, but I happened to be one of those who knew it. And now the appearance at my home of the two men with one of St. Michael's strongest political bosses could only mean that the local machine was falling in line with the rest.

It also meant the syndicate undoubtedly would be powerful enough by the time of the next state convention to put into the governor's mansion the candidate of its choice.

All these thoughts skipped through my mind while Grange was talking. And while they were passing through my mind, I dispassionately considered just what the syndicate was.

It is, as anyone who followed the televised congressional investigation of crime knows, a nationwide federation of professional gamblers, procurers, dope peddlers and racketeers. No decent citizen could feel anything but abhorrence for all that Manetti and Price stood for.

On the other hand my refusal to deal with the syndicate would merely transfer its interest to some other candidate who was willing to accept its backing. And if it was inevitable that a syndicate-backed governor was going to administer our state, I might as well be it.

I asked, "What does this backing involve?"

Tony Manetti spoke in a slurred voice which still contained a trace of Sicilian accent. "We're willing to drop two hundred grand into the campaign kitty."

The amount startled me, for the dark man mouthed it as casually as I would mention a dime.

I said, "How did you happen to pick me?"

"I sold them," Grange said. "You're a natural. Who else in the state can pull in the independent vote and at the same time draw machine backing? With the rubes you have a reputation as a crusader. To the smart boys you have a reputation for . . . cooperation. How could we lose?"

I asked, "What sort of cooperation would be expected of me?"

Arnold Price drawled, "Nothing much, Kenneday. We might ask for a few appointments. The police commissioners of St. Michael and Tailor City, for instance."

"I see," I said dryly.

I toyed with the thought of refusing point blank, as my ability to compromise didn't extend to turning the state over to a gang of murderers. But I only toyed with it. The next instant I thought of a number of justifications for accepting syndicate backing.

The first was the argument that if I refused, some other candidate was bound to accept and the state would be no better off than if I accepted. The second was that any promises I made to a gang of killers I was not morally bound to keep. I told myself I could never get into the governor's mansion without syndicate backing, but once there I could stop being a politician and start being a statesman. I decided I would administer the state government to the best of my ability if I managed to get elected, even if it meant being kicked out of office after four years.

I said, "I would appreciate your backing for the governorship very much, gentlemen. And you won't find me ungrateful."

After the three men left I felt rather proud of myself. It pleased me to think Manetti and Price would go to great trouble and expense to put me in office, only to discover after election that they had made the mistake of backing an honest man. Somehow the situation seemed to counterbalance all the moral compromises I had made in the past in order to gain votes.

But I might have known syndicate representatives wouldn't be naive enough to be satisfied with mere verbal assurance that I'd cooperate after election. I should have been prepared for the next move. My only excuse for being caught by surprise is that I underestimated Manetti and Price.

In the month since my meeting with Tim Grange and the two syndicate men, political forces have been whipped into line, and it's now a practical certainty my nomination for governor will pass on the first ballot at the state convention. Meantime, I still have my job as district attorney to perform.

I wish I could resign tomorrow, for finally I am confronted with a decision for which I can find no self-justification by calling it practical politics.

I've known all along, of course, that the syndicate's political maneuvering is merely a means to an end, and the end is opening wide the whole state to gambling, vice, narcotics and every other illegal racket into which it can get its fingers. Some local opposition by racketeers who preferred to remain independent was inevitable, and the syndicate's solution to such opposition is murder.

There's already been one gang killing in St. Michael County.

My old friend, Big Joey Martin, who was my first contact with the System. The underworld rumor is that Big Joey refused to throw in with the syndicate, and his death was a warning to others who might be slow about falling in line.

It's only a rumor though. There is no evidence pointing at anyone, which might be expected in a murder arranged by so efficient an organization. We have a body, three .45 calibre slugs from a gun which is probably at the bottom of the river, and nothing else but the rumor.

But even though I haven't enough evidence to justify an arrest, I know why Big Joey died. It's been bad enough to carry that knowledge in my mind, but my present situation is impossible.

An hour ago I got a phone call from Tony Manetti, who asked a small favor. The publicity over Big Joey Martin's killing was a bad thing only six months before election, he said, and it would be smart to avoid any such future publicity. He wanted to know how well I knew the coroner.

When I told him Howard Jordan was a personal friend of mine, he said arrangements had been made with Jordan to find accident the cause of death in the case of Willie Tamm, president of the Dock Workers' Local. There was the matter of paying the coroner a small fee for his trouble, however, Manetti went on, and he wondered if I would be willing to relay this fee on if he had it dropped by my office.

The meaning behind his words was unmistakable. The syndicate is not satisfied with my verbal promise to cooperate. It wants me involved beyond backing out in the compounding of a murder.

For you see, Willie Tamm is not yet dead.

Manetti gave me one hour to think things over and call him back. But, in the face of the horror of the situation, I can hardly think.

The insidiousness of the thing is appalling. If I refuse, I'm certain Willie Tamm will not die, for Manetti could hardly afford to go ahead with a murder he'd discussed with an uncooperative district attorney. At the same time, he hasn't run any risk, since I can hardly charge him with a crime which remains uncommitted.

But if I refuse to cooperate, I know my hope for the governorship is gone forever. Without putting it into actual words, Manetti has served notice that I'll become governor on the syndicate's terms, or not at all. Almost certainly, arrangements have been made with Coroner Jordan for some kind of deposition confessing I paid him to cover up a murder. A deposition which they'll keep as a secret weapon to force my future cooperation.

I wonder how huge a sum the syndicate had to pay Jordan to get him to risk his own neck.

The thing which makes it impossible is that I'm an honest man. My moral precepts are probably as high as those of any other member who attends my church. Never in my life have I accepted a penny of dishonest money. My worst sin has been accepting the compromises any practical politician must make if he expects to stay in public life.

How could I possibly have drifted into such an untenable position? Obviously I can't be party to a deliberate murder.

On the other hand, until an hour ago the governorship was right within my grasp.

How can I turn it loose now?

In the Introduction I referred to a loss of innocence reflected in the short stories of this twenty-five-year series. Something of that innocence can be found in this story from the 1956 anthology. No thought here that the policeman is a repressive force: he is portrayed with warmth and understanding; he is shown to have compassion and to be deeply troubled by the requirements of his job. His conscience jabs him and he has a well-developed sense of right and wrong. This story appeared originally in The Saturday Evening Post. *Am I wrong in thinking that the magazine or another like it would not publish this story today?*

WILLIAM FAY

The Conscience of the Cop

The man who had attempted to hold up the liquor store had fallen forward when Heidig shot him and he was dead on the sidewalk in the sweet summer evening. He wore a lightweight suit, cream-toned and attractive, with the crease still fresh at the back of the pants. Cars were stopping along Eighth Avenue.

"You did it real nice and quick," the other detective said to George Heidig. "You made no mistakes."

"Thank you, Morris."

"You're two-thirds of a sergeant already," Morris said, not in envy, but in professional appraisal. It was the way the thing had happened. Morris, as the driver of the car, had of necessity taken ten or fifteen seconds longer getting to the scene. "You were very good, George."

"I was tremendous," Heidig said.

He was still taking deep breaths, looking down at the man he had shot. *About my own age,* Heidig thought; *thirty years old— thirty-one?* He didn't look like a thief or a punk. His leghorn hat, with a gay red ribbon around it, had rolled as far as the curb. He had reddish-brown hair that made him look Irish. The lights from the liquor store kept the pavement so bright you could count the dead man's freckles. Heidig could not see his victim's face, but neither could he forget the one brief glimpse of it that had been stenciled in his mind. He could hear the sirens of two patrol cars, loud and insistent, almost here.

"His name was Harrigan," Morris Lerner said. "Gerald F. Harrigan, accordin' to a light-and-gas bill that he should have paid three months ago. Three twenty—the other number's smudged here—Columbus Avenue. That would be uptown. You all right?"

"I'm all right, Morris," Heidig said. "I hope I'm all right. I never killed a man before."

Now the crowd was very big, encircling the body that lay in the vivid light. The uniformed cops from the patrol cars established a circle of privacy. Morris Lerner had picked up the small automatic and marked it, as routine required. There was nothing to do but wait for the specialists from Homicide. The bright, gay hat of the dead man had been trampled.

"You want a cigarette?" Morris asked.

"Thanks," Heidig said.

He was steady enough. He hadn't been too scared through the whole episode. There was just this feeling that kept growing and getting bigger inside of him. It was half past eleven then.

Heidig got home at ten minutes after one. A big breeze swept the apartment, raising the curtains like summer skirts, as though you were sailing up the Hudson on an excursion boat. It was a new apartment in a downtown municipal project. The space was right and the price was right: four and a half rooms, $77.50. You could look south to the Brooklyn Bridge or north beyond the United National. Sheila had left a light on in the living room so he wouldn't slide on the rattan rug. The three kids were asleep, lightly covered, in the larger of the bedrooms, one window closed, because the breeze from the north could get so muscular, even in July. Heidig heard the refrigerator click, then begin to hum in its easy way. *I'd like a beer,* he thought.

"George?" Sheila called.

He walked in, carrying his can of beer and an opener. She had snapped on the lamp at her side of the bed and she was sitting up, resting on one arm, watching him, squinting and looking pretty, her hair in curlers. They hadn't had a real live argument in many weeks. Things were good with them. Heidig sat down on the bed, holding the beer can and the opener in one hand, putting his face into the warm, soft groove of her neck and shoulder.

"Hello, Dutchman," Sheila said. "You and your beer." She held him close.

"Hello," Heidig said, very softly, his face still against her, but he didn't say "Hello, Irish," in the usual way. There was a difference tonight. The word projected too easily the man on the sidewalk and his reddish hair and the clear Celtic freckles. Heidig used the opener on the beer can, forcing a small triangular hole in the tin. He passed the beer to Sheila, who took one determined swallow. It was a kind of ritual they had. She said she never minded him smelling of go-to-bed beer if she had a little bit of it herself. He sat watching her.

"You very tired?" she said.

"Not so tired."

"What then?"

"We had a little action tonight—Morris and I."

She put her hands behind her head, straightening some of the pins he had disarranged, her full lips pale from a lack of rouge on them, her eyes very watchful.

"Yes, George?"

"I killed a man," he said. "A stick-up on Eighth Avenue."

"Sweet, merciful Saviour," Sheila said. All the color was gone from her face. She moved instinctively closer. "It might have been you."

"It wasn't me. It was him. He looked like your brother Frank."

She watched him carefully, knowing the trouble was real. He had never come home like this before. "You want to talk about it, don't you, George?"

"I think so," Heidig said.

She got out of bed, and she looked very good in her nylon nightgown. Heidig thought, *I'll be dead when I don't notice that.* She put three cups of water in a small percolator; then she walked with it to the stove and turned on a burner.

"Excuse me," Sheila said, then went in and looked at the children, as though it were a necessary thing to do. She came back. "Go ahead and talk," she told him softly.

"This fellow was coming out of the liquor store," Heidig said. "He had some money in one hand—twelve lousy dollars, it turned out—and an automatic pistol in the other. I was very close to him when I shot him."

Sheila put three measured tablespoons of coffee in the top of the percolator. "You're a policeman," she said. "This man had a gun. Why is it complicated, George?"

"I can't exactly say," he told her. "Or if I do know how to say it, I don't want to—yet." *Did I give him enough of a chance?* Heidig wondered. *Would he have shot me if I hadn't got him?*

"Please George."

"It's trying to remember things as they really were that has me all mixed up. Something happened in one second and I don't know yet if I was right or wrong. All I know is—and this is the strange part—I liked him."

Sheila stared at him. "But that's insane, isn't it? How can you like or dislike a man in one second?"

"You get an impression," Heidig said. "A guy is dead and you remember. I'm stuck with that. His name was Harrigan. He had a wife and two kids."

"That's laying it on," Sheila said. "Anyone can have two kids. Did he love them the way you love ours? Would he go out with a gun in his hand if he was what he should have been?"

"He had no criminal record, far as we know. I learned that much. He was a very tidy dresser; he'd make Morris or me look like a bum. And all he had on him was a light-and-gas bill, three months overdue. He had a silly grin on his face, like Frank sometimes, when Mable finds out he's been drinkin'."

"Did you see his wife and children, George?"

"Oh, no! Somebody else checks that; then calls it in. That much is routine. The liquor-store clerk was no help. He was old and too scared. There's just the one thing has its teeth in my conscience."

"Say what you want to say, George."

"I keep thinking he wouldn't have shot me," Heidig said slowly, almost recitatively. "That he'd have dropped the gun and the stinkin', petty-larceny twelve dollars on the sidewalk, if I'd waited.

I keep thinking that perhaps I murdered him, and I'd feel like I stuck a knife in you and the kids and spat on God, if that was true."

"Stop it!" Sheila screamed.

So he stopped. She fell against him, and they held together swaying, slowly rocking in intimate expression of things they felt but could not speak. Her eyes were wet against his face, and Heidig, who had never before been weak, was grateful to have it this way.

"I've got tomorrow off," he said. "I'll look around. I'll find out things."

"You're tormenting yourself, that's all; and you're imagining."

"I've got to know," he said.

"But you couldn't have done anything too wrong. Not you, George."

"I wonder," Heidig said.

It was almost noon and the sun had climbed like a hot balloon. There wasn't a breeze worth a sick man's sneeze on Columbus Avenue. The Harrigans lived in one of a group of flats above a vegetable market, a shoe-repair shop and a corner bar and grill. The smell of bananas was richer than perfume in the heat. Heidig pushed a downstairs buzzer under a mail slot labeled HARRIGAN. There was no response. The downstairs door was open. Heidig walked up a flight and knocked on Apartment C. He waited. He tried the next apartment—B. No answer. Only A responded.

"Yes, sir?"

"Do you know the Harrigans?"

"I know them." She was a thin, tired woman in a house dress. There was captive sweat in the lines of her neck. She pushed her hair back, watching him. "Well?"

"I'm a policeman."

"I can't help you. What was their business isn't mine."

She closed the door. Heidig was going to obstruct this action with his foot, but he did not. The time he was spending on his day off was his own. He didn't want a lot of shouting in the hall. The information he had on the Harrigans was preliminary and brief. The widow had been notified at this address. She had two children and was employed in some capacity at a place called The Coppe

Door, on Sixty-third Street. Heidig had a feeling a man's biography could best be rendered by neighbors who wanted to talk. And there were always enough of these.

He walked downstairs to the soiled street and the griddle heat of the day. The woman who had refused to speak with him was at her window, watching. *I'm an enemy already,* Heidig thought. The vegetable man sat half asleep under a patched green awning. Heidig walked away from the strong smell of bananas, deciding to try the bar and grill. It said McBRIDE's on the window.

"I'll have a glass of beer, please," Heidig said.

"Well, it's about the right weather for it." The bartender filled an eight-ounce goblet. "There now."

It was a real nice glass of beer in nice surroundings, Heidig thought. McBride's, like a thousand saloons in modest neighborhoods, had the restful substantiality not otherwise available to a majority of its clients. It wasn't air-conditioned, but the fans turned effectively, almost silently under the spotless, corrugated, white-painted tin of the ceiling. There were a half-dozen men at the bar, two of them reading the morning papers. Most of them looked at Heidig without special interest, yet he knew that talk had been suspended. The bartender came back, carrying empty glasses. He was a man in his thirties, tall, proficient, cool-looking.

"Fill it again, sir?"

"I wouldn't mind," said Heidig, watching him. "You know a family next door—name of Harrigan?"

"Jerry."

There were intimacy and feeling in the way the one word had been spoken. It controlled the moment. The total attention of each man present was involved. They all looked at Heidig. The bartender stared at his own hands, flat on the bar—studiously, as though he had never seen them before.

"Are you a cop?"

"That's right," Heidig said. "It's why I asked the question. I figured you might have known him."

"Know Jerry?" The bartender's smile was wistful. He turned to the others present. "Did we know the sweetest guy uptown?"

"Lay off the corn and the sirup," Heidig demanded. But the weight of despair was with him. It was like a gamble taken and lost. You couldn't alter what might be true by screaming aloud that it was barroom sentimentality. You couldn't whine like a child for a change of rules when you found what you feared you might find.

"You asked about a friend of mine," the bartender said. "I didn't ask you." He took Heidig's fifty-cent piece and rang up two beers on the register. "We're supposed to be happy because a cop shot Jerry dead?"

"I didn't say that." *Easy now,* he warned himself. "How long did you know Harrigan?"

"Six, seven months. He was from Massachusetts. He came down lookin' for a break. A helluva break he got—him with his talent."

"What do you mean 'talent'?"

"He was a streamlined Jackie Gleason," the bartender said. "Ask them. Ask anybody here that knew the guy. Laugh? . . . How about that, Phil?"

"I don't want to talk about it," said the man named Phil. "Not to the cops. Not to anybody. What's personal is personal. You mind?"

"That's up to you," Heidig said.

"Exactly, officer. It's up to me."

The man named Phil was bulbously large. He swamped the bar stool that supported him. His thighs made his capacious pair of khaki pants look tighter than bologna skins. The sweat worked through the weave of his T shirt. His heavy hands were eloquent. For a man who didn't wish to talk, he managed to say a lot.

"Do you play the piano, officer?"

"No," Heidig said.

"Or sing?" Phil said.

"Look, I'm not being questioned here."

"You asked us if Jerry Harrigan had talent, didn't you?"

Heidig's silence conceded that. He took another swallow of beer. It tasted less good than before. The heat of the day was rising. Heidig's head began to ache. The man named Phil controlled the stage.

"Jerry'd sit there at the piano—any night. You'd think his fingers were part of the keyboard. Name it, he would play it—sweet, hot, boogie, the Eyetalian mambo. Sing like his mother was a nightingale or a bird. Tell stories? Even a cop'd laugh, fall down in a stitch when Harrigan cut loose. It's just he never got a break. Know what I mean? Three months ago he came in second on teevee talent contest. Everybody in this bar here saw the show. Jerry was robbed o' first prize. Good times or bad, he'd wear that grin like it was painted on his face. Good times or—"

"All right, hold it," Heidig said.

"You don't like the way I tell it?"

"I get the idea. He was the sweetest kid since Little Boy Blue, but he carried a gun last night. He held up a liquor store. Why? Did he work for a living?"

"Show business. That's what we told you," Phil said. "Happy-go-lucky an' quick with the buck. Is that a crime?"

"Who supported his kids?"

"Ask his ghost," said Phil, with a great sense of theater. He was a gifted, dangerous cornball, Phil, and Heidig suddenly hated him—almost as much as he was learning to hate himself. "Ask the cop who shot him dead."

It hurt very much, and Heidig thought, *They're ahead of me.* He turned to the bartender then, hoping to change the trend of the evidence. "Did you know Harrigan's wife?"

"I'd see her around," the bartender said, "but she never came in here. A big straw blonde, she could knock down a wall. Jerry never talked about her. He never laid his troubles on the bar."

"She was no help to his career," Phil said.

Heidig didn't want to talk to him. He turned again to the bartender. "There's nobody at the apartment. Where would I find her? Where would I find the kids?"

"Try the old lady," he was advised.

"Whose old lady?"

"Jerry's mother-in-law. The name's Delaney. Around the corner. The first house, with the tailor in the basement."

Heidig walked out into the thumping glare. The sun was high enough to fry the streets and shrink the shade. A truck, half stacked with kegs of beer, had parked outside McBride's place in a bus-stop area. The driver, awash with sweat, walked around to the side of the truck. Heidig knew him from other neighborhoods.

"I'll only be a few minutes, George."

"It's all right," Heidig said.

He pushed the downstairs button where it said DELANEY. The stairs were steep in the converted brownstone house. It was cool and dark and damp within the narrow stairwell.

"Mrs. Delaney?"

"Who is it?"

"I'm a policeman, Mrs. Delaney."

She stood in the open doorway, and you couldn't say that she was fat, because there wasn't enough of her. She was round, small-boned, erect. Her eyes were a blue that Heidig had never seen before, and they were very beautiful.

"Can I help you?"

He stepped inside. The inevitable summer dust danced in slanted sunlight that the shades could not exclude. There were two kids standing near the window—small boys, anywhere from four to six. They wore nothing but shorts and sneakers in the heat, but they looked healthy, like boys at a summer camp. They kept watching him with such alert and friendly interest that Heidig was obliged to look away. There was a small oak table in the center of the room, polished and clean. There was a worn rug on the floor and on the walls he could see the treasures of the respectable Irish poor, a "God Bless Our Home" in lacy lettering, a picture of the Sacred Heart.

"Won't you sit down, officer?"

"The Sixteenth Precinct—West Forty-seventh Street," he said, avoiding any disclosure of his name. He sat down. "About last night," he said.

"Let's remember the children and not say what it wouldn't be right to say," Mrs. Delaney reminded him. She sat at the table.

"Yes, ma'am," Heidig said. "The fact is I'd like to talk with the children's mother—if that's possible."

Mrs. Delaney placed one hand on the table. "My daughter isn't here." She looked cautiously at the children, then leaned forward. "A stranger might think—he might image Mary didn't care much, not to be here at a time like this."

"He might, at that," said Heidig. "Anyone might." He took out a large, sodden handkerchief and wiped his face. "You mind if the children stepped into another room, Mrs. Delaney?"

"But there's only this room. This and the kitchen there."

"M'm'm'm," he said. "Well, could they step outside?"

She looked at him appealingly. "Into the street? With all the talk that's going on about what happened? With them not prepared yet for the things they'd hear?"